A MIXTURE OF MISCHIEF

ALSO BY ANNA MERIANO

Love Sugar Magic: A Dash of Trouble
Love Sugar Magic: A Sprinkle of Spirits

LOVE SUGAR MAGIC

A MIXTURE OF MISCHIEF

ANNA MERIANO

WALDEN POND PRESS

An Imprint of HarperCollinsPublishers

Walden Pond Press is an imprint of HarperCollins Publishers. Walden Pond Press and the skipping stone logo are trademarks and registered trademarks of Walden Media, LLC.

Love Sugar Magic: A Mixture of Mischief
Text copyright © 2020 by Anna Meriano
Illustrations copyright © 2020 by Mirelle Ortega
All rights reserved. Printed in the United States of America.

ISBN 978-0-06-291590-0

Typography by Sarah Nichole Kaufman
19 20 21 22 23   PC/LSCH   10 9 8 7 6 5 4 3 2 1

First Edition

To the readers, and my whole publishing family.
Thanks, y'all.

CHAPTER 1
SO MUCH TO LEARN

Amor y Azúcar Panadería had closed its doors for the night, but inside the warm kitchen, Leo Logroño's work was just beginning.

"I'm ready, Mamá," she said, setting down her knife and wiping her hands on her apron, leaving dark wet streaks amid the generous dusting of flour.

Leo's mother perched on a stool in the corner near the large bakery ovens. She appeared to be focused on the day's receipts, but Leo could see that her mother's eyes were following her every move. "Don't tell me about it," she said, waving a hand toward the oven and lifting her papers closer to her face to hide her smile. "This is your *independent* baking test."

Leo took a deep breath and nodded. She lifted her tray carefully, forcing her eyes off her six oblong dough loaves so she could watch her step. Should she have made the loaves smaller? Had she given them enough time to rise so their insides would be light and fluffy? Her dough looked all right, and the tiny piece she'd snuck into her mouth, once she'd finished mixing and kneading it, tasted all right— much better than the first time she had tried to make this recipe from memory.

But still, Leo wondered if it would be enough to pass Mamá's standards. She slid her tray into the oven, set the timer and steamer for ideal crusty loaves, and breathed a small sigh of relief. If nothing else, she'd gotten this batch into the oven without dropping it, unlike the last one.

Leo had spent weeks pestering Mamá to let her take on more work in the bakery, to give her a job in the kitchen with her older sisters instead of always sticking her behind the cash register. That's how they had come to their current agreement: if Leo could bake a batch of the bakery's basic bread loaf from memory, all by herself, then Mamá would put her on rotation to work in the kitchen. This was Leo's third attempt, not counting one disastrous

kneading session in the kitchen at home. She had
started today's dough just before the bakery closed,
letting it rise while she helped her sisters clean and
shut down the shop. The wait had made her hopes
rise too, and now she felt ready to burst with antic-
ipation.

"How do they look?" she asked, bouncing a little
on the balls of her feet.

"We'll have to see when they come out," Mamá
said, but her eyes twinkled, and Leo's chest loosened. She climbed onto the second stool next to
Mamá and let out a tired puff of breath, wiping wild
tendrils of escaped hair off her forehead and back
under her baseball cap. Sometimes her older sisters
got away with tight ponytails and buns in the bakery, but Leo's hair needed extra containment.

"You know, if you start working during business hours, you won't get much of a break," Mamá
reminded her. "There's always a batch to take out of
the oven, or a new one to start mixing, or—"

"I know!" Leo laughed. "But since I won't have
you watching me and making me nervous, I won't
need a break."

Mamá clicked her tongue. "I don't know what
you're talking about. I've just been going over the
books." She conjured a mechanical pencil out of thin

air and made a note in the margins of the paper in front of her just to prove her point.

Leo copied Mamá's hand motion, a pinch of her fingers and a flick of her wrist, imagining that she too had the bruja power of manifestation. Second-born daughters in the family—like Mamá, and like Leo's sixteen-year-old sister, Marisol— could make small objects appear and disappear as easily as first-borns could manipulate emotions and third-borns could communicate with spirits from el Otro Lado.

As the fourth-born daughter, the first of her kind in generations of Rose Hill brujas, Leo didn't yet know exactly what her special power would be, though she suspected it might have something to do with her ability to see the veil between this world and el Otro Lado. She had discovered that power in January, when her friend Caroline had accidentally thrown open a gate between the world of the living and the world of the dead.

The problem was, being able to see the veil wasn't the most exciting kind of power. Sometimes, if Leo concentrated really hard, she could find the shadowy, shimmery veil and poke her fingers through it, but it wasn't nearly as useful a power as making objects from nothing.

"I know I can be a real baker," Leo said, eyes on the oven door. Everyone else helped in the kitchen, even Marisol, who hated spending time away from her friends, and Alma and Belén, who were still in ninth grade. Just because she was young didn't mean she couldn't do the same. Mamá was giving Leo a chance to prove that she was old enough to take on more responsibility. It was the chance Leo had been waiting for. She just hadn't realized it would be so scary.

Mamá reached across the gap between the stools to give Leo's shoulder a squeeze. "Always in such a hurry to grow up," she said. Then she jumped to her feet. "Well, come on. We've left a mess, and real bakers clean up after themselves."

By the time Leo had wiped her work space, washed and dried all her dishes, and returned everything to its proper place, the air was thick with its normal daytime smell of warm yeast and flour. She paced in front of the glass oven door as her timer ticked down, peeking in at the lonely-looking tray in the big empty belly of the oven. She let out a squeal of excitement when she finally pulled out the tray and saw six beautiful golden bolillos, the crusty bread that made for a perfect side dish as well as the very best sandwiches.

"They look wonderful," Mamá confirmed, and she picked up one of the small hot loaves with her bare hand, something Leo would have gotten in trouble for. "Ready to try it?" She ripped the bolillo in half and offered one steaming end to Leo. On Mamá's nod, Leo bit into her piece, teeth crunching through the outside and sinking into the soft middle. Buttery, fresh, and hot, the bolillo tasted like victory on her tongue.

"Well," Mamá said, chewing thoughtfully, "I'd be a fool to argue with that. Consider yourself eligible for back-of-the-house shifts. You can start tomorrow morning if you like."

Leo leaped into the air, bread raised in triumph. Tomorrow was Saturday, which meant she had two full weekend days to practice working alongside her sisters. She was going to be an expert baker in no time!

Mamá held up a warning finger. "You'll start off slow. Bolillos only for now, and just a couple of batches at a time." Her face stayed stern for three seconds before softening. "Good job, 'jita."

"Thank you." Leo couldn't wait to get home and tell her sisters. Isabel would be proud like Mamá, and Alma and Belén would claim not to be surprised. Marisol might pretend to wonder why anyone would celebrate having more work to do, but she'd probably be happy to swap baking for Leo's shifts at the register in the front of the bakery. Leo nibbled her bread while Mamá shut down the oven for the night, her heart glowing like the fading light of the oven heating coils.

But after her third bite, her jubilation faded. Something tasted . . . off.

"Let's bring these home," Mamá said, packing Leo's loaves into a paper bag and rinsing the tray in the oversized sink. "I've been craving capirotada now that it's almost Easter, and these would be perfect for it."

Leo took the bag Mamá offered her with a frown. "Are you sure?" she asked. "Are you positive I got the recipe right?"

"Sure I'm sure," Mamá scanned the kitchen one last time. "Why, what's wrong?"

Leo shrugged. She bit off another piece of the bread. It tasted good, and it tasted like a bolillo, but something was . . . different. It didn't taste like an Amor y Azúcar bolillo. It was like when Mamá bought store-brand cereal—similar, but not quite the same.

"They don't seem exactly right," Leo said. "Should I try again tomorrow night? Maybe I added too much flour and dried out the dough. . . ." She pulled a tiny spiral notebook out of her back pocket, flipping through the pages to see her notes on this batch.

"Wait, 'jita, slow down. You did great," Mamá said. "Is this about nerves? You don't have to start work tomorrow if you don't want to. I know it can be a lot of pressure, but nobody expects you to keep up with everything your older sisters do."

"It's not nerves." Leo shook her head, disappointment weighing down the corners of her mouth. "I want to work in the bakery. I want to be a real baker. But I must have done something wrong. This bolillo doesn't taste like yours."

To her surprise, Mamá laughed. "Well, of course it doesn't. I thought it would be cheating to let you use the mixing bowl."

"The mixing bowl?" Leo knew which bowl Mamá meant—the extra-large wooden one in which Marisol or the twins usually prepared the oversized batches of bolillo dough. Leo had always assumed the bowl was used for its size, not as part of the recipe.

"Indeed," Mamá said, opening one of the tall wooden cabinets and taking out the mixing bowl. "I know that the baking equipment we use doesn't usually make a difference. But this is a family heirloom. There's power in something passed down through the generations."

"Power to make bread tasty?" Leo asked, running

her hand down the smooth side of the bowl. She breathed deep and caught a whiff of her family's spicy magic scent.

Mamá nodded. "Power to make recipes turn out better than perfect."

"So it's another type of relic," Leo said. Tía Paloma, Mamá's younger sister who helped in the bakery and with the magical education of Leo and her sisters, had taught her about objects that could be used to strengthen and channel magic. She just hadn't mentioned that they used a relic to make the daily batches of bread.

"Exactly right." Mamá flipped the lights off, leaving the closed kitchen in darkness except for the dim office light by the back door.

"Why didn't you tell me?"

"It never came up," Mamá said. "It's not like you needed to know it for your baking test."

Leo sighed. As far as Mamá was concerned, Leo never *needed to know* anything.

"You're taking to your lessons well, Paloma says. And your baking has improved so much. You have nothing to worry about, 'jita. Now come on." Mamá held out her hand for Leo to take. "Let's get to bed. We have work in the morning."

* * *

They were most of the way home, and Leo was watching the crescent moon follow them through the streets of Rose Hill when a question popped into her mind.

"Mamá? When I've finished memorizing normal bakery recipes, will I have to memorize all the recipes in the spell book too?" The idea was exciting but daunting. The family spell book was an heirloom as old as the mixing bowl, and each bruja in the family added new magical recipes to the ever-growing compendium.

"Oh no!" Mamá raised her eyebrows and laughed. "The uses of some of the items in the book are so rare, there's no point in knowing them all by heart. That's part of the reason we write them down, so the knowledge doesn't get lost even if it's used infrequently. After you master the basic recipes and spells we use in everyday baking, I might start you on learning spice magic, at least until we figure out what your birth-order power is and whether it requires special training."

"Spice magic?" Leo asked. "But I already learned the spices and herbs. Tía Paloma quizzed me on all their uses."

Mamá turned onto their block and into the Logroño driveway. "Those are the fundamentals, the properties that brujas and brujos of any discipline should know. I'm talking about studying the specific applications of spices in baking spells—the secrets of any family of brujas cocineras."

Leo's heart beat faster—the same as it did anytime she learned about a family secret. "When can I start?"

Mamá's laugh broke the quiet of the stilled engine. "Let's work on making you a 'real baker' first, 'jita. I know you're in a hurry to learn everything at once, but I promise you, there's no rush."

Leo jumped out of the car, barely hearing Mamá's words. She slammed the car door behind her, head already scheming. Starting first thing tomorrow, she would prove she had mastered baking as soon as possible. Then Mamá would have to let her learn all the secrets of spice magic.

Mamá didn't understand how it felt, how Leo always got held back while her older sisters moved ahead. Leo didn't want to be the extra tagalong sister, the unnecessary fourth-born who didn't even have a birth-order power. She wanted to be a bruja, and a baker, and an important part of her family.

She clutched her paper bag of near-perfect bolillos to her chest. This was a good step in the right direction, but she had much more work to do.

CHAPTER 2
PIÑATA COOKIES

By Tuesday, Leo had hatched a plan to improve her baking. Like most of her good ideas, it involved her friends.

"Tricia's birthday falls during spring break next week." Leo's best friend and seat buddy, Caroline, was talking to Brent Bayman as their bus pulled away from Rose Hill Middle School. "And she and her family are going out of town. So we're going to turn tomorrow's snack-club day into a birthday celebration snack club!"

"Sounds delicious!" Brent sat sideways with his legs in the aisle so he could face the girls. "So what are you making? A cake?"

"We haven't decided yet," Leo said. "But it's going to be something spectacular."

Brent glanced back and forth between his friends, excitement waning. "You mean 'spectacular' like a really great flavor and amazing decorations, right? Not 'spectacular' like—" He widened his eyes and wiggled his fingers like he was performing a magic spell.

"We haven't decided yet," Caroline teased, wiggling her fingers back at Brent.

Leo giggled. She wouldn't be surprised if Brent was a bit nervous about his friends using magic. He had been stuck on the wrong end of a mistakenly cast love spell earlier that school year when Leo first discovered the family spell book, and later he had helped track down half a soccer team's worth of spirits who Caroline had accidentally brought back to life—with the help of Leo's family magic—in January. Brent knew more than anyone the problems magic could cause.

To ease his mind, Leo leaned across Caroline and whispered, "We're bringing them to school; they're not going to be anything *too* spectacular."

"Okay," Brent said. "Just please . . . utilize your critical thinking skills." He borrowed the phrase that the sixth-grade teacher, Ms. Wood, had started using when her students made bad choices.

"Critical thinking skills fully activated," Caroline promised. The bus screeched to a halt in front of her and Brent's stop, but she stayed seated as Brent swung his backpack onto his back. "See you tomorrow."

"Thanks for inviting me over, Leo," Caroline said as the bus pulled back into the street. "I love going to your house. There's always something happening!"

The Logroño house was happening, all right. The kitchen in particular was so packed that Leo and Caroline couldn't even start their snack-club baking project until after dinner. First, Daddy made them do all their homework for the next day while he rummaged through the cookie jar for after-school snacks. Then they helped Marisol rip up piles of colored paper for her new art project, which she spread out across the whole kitchen table. Alma and Belén needed opinions on the costumes they were making to wear to a comic convention the next week, and by the time the fashion show was over, Isabel was ready to serve the tostadas Mamá had taught her how to make for dinner.

"This is what I'm going to eat every day when I'm in college next year," Isabel said. "It's way easier than the spaghetti I made last night."

"And somehow less crunchy," Marisol joked, cracking the hard tortilla between her teeth and smirking.

Then there were dishes to do, and by the time Leo and Caroline had the kitchen to themselves, the sun was starting to set and Caroline would have to go soon.

"Okay," Leo said, pulling out bags of flour and sugar from the pantry at lightning speed and lining them up on the counter. "We can still make something spectacular. We just have to make something spectacularly *speedy*."

"I brought something that might help," Caroline said, unzipping the hidden pocket in her sparkly green backpack. "It's for . . . inspiration and clarity, I think." She held up a purplish-blue candle with a slightly crooked base. "I made it myself! At my lesson with your aunt on Wednesday. It's got rosemary, my favorite."

Leo nodded, leaning to inhale the familiar smell of herbs and wax and Caroline's newfound power, a smoky scent that had grown stronger since Tía Paloma had started training Caroline in candle magic. "It looks great. And we need all the help we can get."

The girls had baked together for snack club before, mostly when it was Caroline's turn to bake.

Mr. Campbell was doing his best to stock their pantry and kitchen, but Caroline still came over to Leo's when she needed cake flour, round cake pans, or an icing bag. Since they were founding members of the snack club, along with Tricia Morales and Mai Nguyen, Caroline said that she couldn't show up with cake from a box or slice-and-bake cookies.

"I've got some ideas," Caroline said, pulling her blond hair back into a ponytail before striking a match and holding it up to the candle. The kitchen lights flickered and went out as the candle wick glowed.

"That's not going to be enough light to bake by, girls," Mamá pointed out, peeking in to check their progress.

"Sorry! I'm working on that." Caroline shrugged at Leo with a sheepish grin. "Your aunt says I should be able to light a spelled candle without setting off an actual spell. . . . Hold on." She blew out the candle. The lights came back on.

Caroline stubbornly insisted that blowing out a candle wasn't bad luck in the tradition of her family's magic. Leo respected her friend's difference of opinion, but it still made her cringe. Mamá and Tía Paloma had taught her their superstition as a baby, before she knew about magic. Birthday candles were the only exception. Even Daddy had been trained to douse candles by covering them, and he didn't have any spell-casting abilities at all.

After two more attempts, Caroline managed to light the candle without causing a blackout.

"That's pretty good," Alma said, wandering into the kitchen and pouring two cups of orange juice. "Tía Paloma never taught us that."

Caroline beamed.

"Hurry up," Belén called from the other room. "I need you to find my blue leggings or else this is going to be the worst DragonBlood cosplay ever!" Alma balanced both cups in one hand while she returned the orange juice to the fridge and hurried out of the kitchen.

Leo leaned in and took a deep breath of what she hoped was inspiration and clarity. "So you said you have ideas for the cake?"

"Yes, I watched some YouTube videos and I made a list of options," Caroline took a folded sheet of notebook paper from her pocket. "One: some kind of piñata cake—the ones where you cut into it and candy pours out, or sprinkles. Two: sugar cookies with frosting, because Tricia loves those. Three: puerquitos! It's a little boring, but they're her favorite order from the bakery, and they might be a good idea since we're so short on time. Four . . . something magical."

"We want to eat them in the cafeteria," Leo reminded her friend. "They can't be too magical." Tricia knew about the girls' powers because she had helped them chase down the stray spirits a few months ago, but just because Leo trusted her friends with her family's secret didn't mean she wanted to bring powerful spells to school. "Plus, we sort of promised Brent."

Caroline nodded. "I was just thinking something small," she said, but she pulled a pencil from the side pocket of her backpack and crossed the idea off her list.

Leo considered the other items on the list. "I don't know," she said, "They're all good ideas."

"Mamá doesn't like piñata cakes," Isabel's voice behind her made Leo jump. "She says stuff like that is made for sharing on social media, not for sharing with the people you love. She hates anything *trendy*."

Leo wished she could shoo her sisters away from the kitchen like she shooed her black cat, Señor Gato, with a flick of water from the sink.

Caroline moved her pen to strike that item out too, but Leo held up her hand. "Just because Mamá doesn't like them doesn't mean Tricia wouldn't."

But, a tiny voice in her head reminded her, *it might be better to pick something Mamá will like, to impress her and make her think what a great baker her youngest daughter is.*

She, Caroline, and Isabel stared at the list. Leo's eyes skipped across the remaining items, her brain working as fast as a food processor as she spun them into the beginning of a thought. Slowly, she reached for the tall cone of piloncillo, the dark brown sugar that was used to make Tricia's favorite treat from the bakery: pig cookies.

"Isabel," she said, "could you show Caroline how to make cookie icing? Just the powdered sugar and milk kind. The quicker the better, because we're going to need a lot of different colors."

"Icing is such a hassle," Marisol groaned from the living room.

Caroline rolled her eyes so Leo didn't have to, and smiled. "What are you thinking?"

"I'm thinking this kitchen needs doors," Leo grumbled. "Soundproof doors with big locks, and maybe a warding spell to keep away annoying sisters."

"Leo?" Mamá poked her head into the kitchen just over an hour later. "It's getting late, and I'm sure Mr. Campbell doesn't want to be driving over to pick up Caroline in the middle of the night. What's the estimate on finishing your snack?

Leo squeezed a final series of squiggles across her last cookie. She checked Caroline's tray, which was nearly done and looked neater than Leo's. Her arm was tired from squeezing the bags of icing, but the result looked even better than she had pictured in her head. "Come see," she told Mamá. "We made piñata cookies!"

"Oh." Mamá joined the two girls at the counter and inspected the twenty-six colorful cookies. "That's very festive."

"They just look like piñatas—they don't break open or anything," Leo explained. "We knew you wouldn't like that."

"Well, I'm sure I would like anything you baked," Mamá said, but she looked especially proud as she leaned over to sniff Leo's tray. "The cookies, are they . . . ?"

"Puerquitos!" Leo beamed. "I remembered the recipe perfectly, I'm pretty sure. Tricia loves them, and she loves icing, so we covered them!" The counter was a mess of half-empty icing bags, bright red and yellow and pink and blue. Each pig-shaped cookie sported multicolored lines of icing, looped to mimic the textured paper covering a piñata. "What do you think?"

The corners of Mamá's eyes crinkled with her smile. "I think this is wonderfully creative. You girls have both come a long way with your baking."

"It was mostly Leo." Caroline blushed. "She knows all the recipe secrets. I'm just the assistant."

Leo's chest swelled. "But you're the best at measuring," she reminded her friend. "And remembering to preheat the oven!"

"Well," Mamá said, "I think I'm allowed to be impressed with both of you. I'm sure Tricia will love them. Caroline, do you think you can ask your dad to head this way soon?"

"Of course," Caroline pulled out her phone and quickly typed a message. "Thanks again for having me."

"Thank *you*," Mamá said, patting Caroline's arm. "You're always welcome, especially when your snack-club idea has Leo inventing original recipes. That's the mark of a real baker in training."

Leo beamed down at her piñata puerquitos, pride heating her cheeks and her stomach. Leo had never seen Alma and Belén experiment with baking; they had taken more interest in the candle magic that helped them enhance their gift of communicating with the dead. Marisol wouldn't spend one minute of her free time doing anything related to the family business. Even Isabel saved most of her outside studies for general spellcraft more than inventing recipes.

In the days since she'd passed her test, she had probably made a billion bolillos, and she was proud of how she had fallen into the rhythm of keeping the trays flowing into and out of the oven and the bread flowing into customers' hands and out the door. But this praise from Mamá was special. Leo was on her way to becoming a real baker.

She was still thinking of Mamá's compliment later that night, long after Caroline had left. Leo packed the cookies into a cardboard bakery box and changed into her pajamas. As she brushed her teeth, an idea popped into her head, so exciting it made her spit out her toothpaste immediately and run to Mamá and Daddy's room.

"What's up, Leonora?" Daddy asked, propping his binder of bakery invoices open on the bedspread and tucking his pencil behind his ear.

Leo wiped her mouth on the back of her hand. "Can we put my piñata cookies in the recipe book?" she asked, pleading eyes fixed on Mamá's surprised face.

"Oh." Mamá set down her magazine. "Well, I'm sure the cookies are delicious. . . ."

Leo nodded. She had split one test cookie with Caroline, which still left plenty for the whole class tomorrow.

". . . But," Mamá continued, frowning, "we can't really put it in the spell book if it doesn't cast a unique spell."

The bubble of excitement in Leo's chest popped. Of course. The recipe book was for magical recipes only. But her emotions fizzed right back up again as she thought aloud, "Well, I could put a spell on them. Like, a luck spell. I'm great at those!"

Mamá's smile was soft. "You are, but that wouldn't be an original spell, 'jita."

"Right." Leo sighed.

"Listen, most brujas don't contribute to the book until they've been training for years," Mamá said. "There's no rush."

"Leo, I'll have you know that I have never added a spell to the book, or even cast one, and I turned out okay." Daddy spread his arms and smiled.

But Leo didn't feel any better. "Isabel invented a spell already." She hated being told not to race toward her goals when she could see so clearly that she was barely keeping up.

"I'll tell you what," Mamá said. "During your shift tomorrow, how about we whip up a few batches of your piñata cookies and sell them? Does that sound good to you?"

Leo's gloom vanished and her mouth dropped open. Her own invented treat on the bakery shelves? None of her sisters had ever done that before. "That sounds super-duper extra good!" she shouted, bouncing onto her parents' bed to hug Mamá's propped-up knees. "Can we really?"

"Of course we can," Daddy said, tapping Leo's ponytail with his pencil. "If those cookies taste as good as they look, then it's just good business. And I should know, I happen to be running a very successful business this quarter—maybe you've heard of it? It's the best bakery in all of Texas!"

This time, Leo grinned at her father's joke.

"Oh, one other thing, 'jita," said Mamá. "Paloma's taking the twins out of town for spring break, so you won't have your normal lessons. I was thinking I could give you a quick lesson in spice magic next week. I think you've earned it. And besides, I've learned the hard way that it's usually more trouble to keep you from trying to learn magic on your own than it is to just teach you myself."

Leo's spirits soared. This was the most successful scheme ever. She let Mamá and Daddy wrap her up in a hug before she practically skipped down the hall to her bedroom. She couldn't wait to tell Tricia tomorrow that her special birthday treat would soon be the newest seasonal dessert at Amor y Azúcar. She couldn't wait to tell Caroline that she was moving on to spice magic. Most of all, she couldn't wait for the day when she was grown up and running the bakery with her sisters, juggling magic and sugar and loving every minute of it.

She fell into bed and dreamed of round pig piñatas that spilled sweetness from their broken bellies.

CHAPTER 3
HOPES AND HERBS

In just a few days, Leo's piñata pig cookies became the most popular new item at Amor y Azúcar. They sold so well that, even though Mamá rolled her eyes at all the pictures people kept taking and posting on Twitter and Instagram, she set aside one whole rack in the ovens just to make sure the shelves were stocked. Marisol, on the other hand, jumped at the opportunity to set up an online presence for the bakery, and soon dubbed herself social media manager.

"I don't mean to alarm anyone," Daddy announced at family dinner on Friday, the night before the twins left for their comic convention with Tía Paloma, "but your mamá and I have a special announcement. Your cousin JP is going to spend spring break week here with us while Margarita goes to a conference in Chicago. She'll be dropping him off tomorrow!"

"Hmm, we won't get to see him," Belén said. Alma nodded sadly. JP was thirteen, the nearest in age to Leo of all her cousins, though he usually stuck close to Alma and Belén at family gatherings. Leo hoped he wouldn't be too disappointed to leave his friends in Austin and get stuck in Rose Hill without the twins for spring break. Maybe Caroline could help her make a list of fun activities they could do together. She had lived in Houston, after all, so she would know what things cool kids from big cities liked.

"Huh," Marisol said casually. "I thought you were going to tell us about how you and Daddy were going to buy a new house."

"What?" Mamá looked at Marisol with wide eyes. "How did you—I mean, why do you think that?"

"I started getting a bunch of Realtor ads on the office computer," Marisol said. "And the bakery email had spam from one of those real-estate websites. That's what happens when you search for new houses on the internet. Have you found a place? Are we moving?"

Leo stared at her sisters in shock. A new house had been Mamá's dream for so long that Leo had given up on it actually happening. Mamá and Daddy, meanwhile, shared a nervous glance.

"Wow, the tables have really turned," Marisol teased. "Are you two *hiding things*? Because usually that's my job."

"We . . . didn't want to get your hopes up," Daddy said. "In case things don't work out. But yes, we're hoping to make it happen. Soon."

"We were planning to wait until the end of summer to see how we do in the slow season," Mamá said, "but with business doing so well lately, we think it's time."

Leo clapped her hands. "Will the new house be closer to school?" she asked. She would love to be in walking or biking distance from Caroline and Brent.

"Can we still share a room?" Alma and Belén spoke in unison.

"Are you sure we can afford this, even with college and everything?" Isabel frowned.

"Does this mean you can help me buy my car too?" Marisol asked.

"Yes; yes; we'll make it work; and probably not." Daddy answered the questions in rapid succession. "Sorry, Marisol, but if anyone's getting a car, it'll be Isabel, so she can come home from San Antonio next year whenever she needs to."

As Marisol grumbled about the unfairness and Mamá talked about all the things they'd been looking for in a new house, Leo held in a secret smile. Daddy said this was all happening because business was good. Business was good because of her cookies—sure, it had only been a few days, but Leo was still happy to take credit for the recent business. Plus tomorrow Mamá was going to teach her spice magic, and then later she would get to show her cousin her town.

This was going to be the best spring break ever.

It came as a surprise, then, when Leo woke up the next morning feeling unsettled, with a bad dream hovering at the edge of her memory. The anxious feeling refused to budge, even when Leo rubbed the sleep from her eyes and shook her head. She checked the corners of her bedroom before throwing off the covers. She felt like she was being watched.

Leo was still dazed when Marisol sleepily rattled the bathroom door. Leo was so surprised that she jumped and dropped her toothbrush in the sink.

"You're up early," Marisol said when Leo let her in. "Excited about your magic lesson?"

Leo just sighed, rinsed, and left the bathroom to her sister.

"Oh, good." Isabel caught hold of Leo's ponytail in the hallway. "I was about to wake you up. Mamá wants to get an early start so that you have time for your lesson before JP gets here. Do you want me to braid your hair?"

Leo shook her head and slipped out of Isabel's reach. Determined to shake her bad morning mood, she pulled on a sunny yellow shirt and headed to the kitchen.

"Thanks for telling me," Mamá said, telephone held between her ear and her shoulder. "And drive safe. Please make sure the girls spend some time learning from the coven up there. They can take one day away from that convention." Mamá hung up the phone and smiled when she saw Leo. "Good morning, 'jita! Ready to get going?"

"Was that Tía Paloma?" Leo asked. "What's wrong?"

"Nothing's wrong," Mamá said, waving her hand. "She was just letting me know that they were on the road. And it seems like they're starting some new construction at Donatello's, over by the freeway. They passed it on the way out of town."

Leo shrugged. She knew the empty building with

the fading cursive sign. Why would Tía Paloma think it was worth interrupting her road trip to tell Mamá?

"They're not reopening that old pizza place, are they?" Daddy asked, entering the kitchen blowing on a cup of coffee. "The crust was like cardboard. If the town wants pizza so badly, I bet we could cook up a decent one."

"Now, now." Mamá patted Daddy's shoulder. "No reason to get into a competition with another local business. We're not trying to run anyone out of a job."

"So they're really reopening?" Marisol asked, walking in and stealing a sip of Daddy's coffee before he could stop her. "I used to love that place when I was little."

"No, someone else bought the building." Mamá picked up her own coffee mug and took a long sip. "Some store called Honeybees."

Leo felt a shiver at the name, and the sense that she was forgetting something important grew stronger. Had there been bees in her dream last night? She couldn't remember, and the frustration felt like an out-of-reach itch as her family finished breakfast and piled into the car.

When they reached the bakery, Leo moved

automatically to her work station, pulling out the mixing bowl to start the first batch of bolillos, still looking over her shoulder for some unpleasant surprise.

"Leo?" Mamá put a hand on her shoulder. "What are you doing?"

"I don't know," Leo's voice whined. She wondered if she was getting sick; that could explain why she felt so terrible.

"Come to the office, 'jita. Isabel and Marisol can handle the bolillos today; I want to get you started on spice magic." Mamá looked down at Leo, her mouth pressing into a worried line. "Unless you're not up for it? We can always—"

"No!" Leo didn't know if magic lessons could sweeten her crab-apple mood, but she knew she would feel a lot worse if she missed her chance to learn. "I'm ready. Let's go."

She followed Mamá into the bakery office, where shelves of cookbooks and binders lined the walls. Mamá's and Daddy's desks normally overflowed with papers and receipts and delivery order forms; today, though, Mamá had cleared her desk, and on it she placed two glass jars from the spice rack and an odd-shaped object covered in a silk cloth.

The mystery on the desk made Leo forget about her bad feeling, just a bit.

"All right," Mamá said. "An introduction to spice magic. First: everything you've learned with your tía is going to form the basis of what you're doing today."

Leo nodded. She had studied all the magical properties and uses of different herbs and spices for Tía Paloma's quiz. "Am I going to have to memorize more spices?" she asked. She wouldn't mind, but it wasn't quite the excitement she had hoped for to get her mind off her forgotten dream.

Mamá shook her head. "Spice magic will draw on what you know, but it works a little differently. A last resort, a cheat even, for brujas like us. You've seen how our recipes come together: a mix of baking and herbs and candles and magical items and different sources of sugar. The reason we combine so many different processes is because of the specific challenges we have, making spells that are also edible. That is the *spice problem*." She opened the lids of the two glass jars, wrapped her hands around the labels, and held them out to Leo. "What's in these?" she asked.

Leo leaned forward and sniffed. "Cinnamon," she said, pointing at the first one. "Good for strengthening spells or protection. Good for winter recipes." She leaned over the second jar. "Peppermint. Helps with stomach problems, used for general healing spells, and very strong in flavor. Mamá, these are too easy."

Mamá laughed. "You'll be glad they're so distinctive in a minute. Now, imagine I had a healing recipe for mint chocolate cookies. And I wanted it to be extra strong, and a little protection couldn't hurt either. Could I add cinnamon to the recipe?"

Leo hesitated. She knew by Mamá's teacher tone of voice that she shouldn't answer yes. "I guess . . . I guess it would taste kind of funky?" she said.

Mamá nodded. "Right. And let's say I wanted to add lemongrass to prevent illness as well. And lavender, for relaxation."

Leo made a face. "You wouldn't be making very good cookies anymore."

"Exactly." Mamá set the jars on the desk with a clink. "There's an extra dimension to our spells, one that requires flexibility and creativity and a strong list of potential substitutes, like how honey can serve some of the same purposes in a spell that cinnamon normally would. But sometimes you just really need the power of one thing with the taste of another. And *that* is how we discovered spice magic."

Mamá pulled the silk cloth off the desk with a flourish, revealing a black stone bowl and a round stone tool. Now that it was uncovered, Leo could smell the magic of the molcajete even before she leaned close to examine it. "Another heirloom?" she guessed.

Mamá's smile matched her own. "Your great-grandmother would use this practically every day to make masa, salsa, or ground spices. We can buy all of those things at the store or make them in the food processor now, but the power of the molcajete still helps when we need to call on spice magic. The bowl stores power from everything it touches, and we can use that property to transfer power from one type of spice into another. This also lets us combine the powers of herbs to strengthen one particular property that they share. Let me show you how to get started. . . ."

Mamá demonstrated a few different motions with the grinding stone, and soon Leo had had gotten the hang of infusing peppermint with the power of cinnamon and vice versa, grinding a tiny pinch of one spice into the bowl to release its power and then adding the second to absorb it.

Mamá checked the clock. "We have time for at least one more trial before your aunt gets here with JP," she said. "Do you want to keep trying with these two, or use a new spice?"

Leo considered a moment, and an idea popped

into her head. Good thing Tía Paloma had drilled those lists of spice uses into her head so carefully. "Can I check the cabinet?" she asked.

"Sure, help yourself. I'll just check on your sisters, and you can show me what you come up with."

Mamá left, and Leo rummaged through the bakery's supply of spices until she found the jars she wanted. She returned to the molcajete and added a tiny pinch of rosemary. Leo rocked the grinding stone slowly, breathing evenly as it pushed the spice around the bowl. The stone warmed in her hand. When she had finished thirteen clockwise and seven counterclockwise turns, she added a handful of bay leaves, crushing them down to dull green dust.

"About ready?" Mamá asked.

Leo tilted the molcajete. "I'm not sure. I think so."

Mamá licked her finger and dipped it into the bowl, bringing a smidge of the powder to her tongue. A smile broke over her face as she nodded. "Bay leaf infused with rosemary, and you kept the power of both. Insight and clarity, an interesting combination. Have you been having bad dreams?"

Leo ducked her head. "I thought I had one last night. I thought I might figure out what it meant."

Mamá gestured at the bowl, so Leo dipped her finger in and tasted her infusion. The powder stuck to the roof of her mouth and she coughed, but she felt a jolt, like cold water in her face. The fog in her brain did seem to clear, at least a little bit. But she still couldn't remember her dream. She looked at Mamá and shook her head.

"Well, it was good work anyway," Mamá said. "I think that's all we have time for right now, but once you get the concept, it's just a matter of practice, so the next time we have an order that needs any spice magic we can put you in charge. You'll get the hang of it quickly, I'm sure."

Leo beamed. Mamá shook Leo's dream spice into a tiny plastic bag, then wrapped the molcajete in its silk. "Put the spices back, will you? Better not to leave them out when a member of the nonmagical side of your family is about to arrive." She flipped the office light on her way out the door.

In the suddenly dim room, Leo froze in place. Even though light still streamed through the doorway, the darkness paralyzed her, and the eyes she had felt watching her all day seemed to pierce holes in the back of her neck.

A voice, a memory, echoed in her brain as last night's dream finally came back to her.

"Is that any way to treat your abuelo Logroño?"

CHAPTER 4
VISITORS

In a corner of her bedroom that had been empty a minute before, there now stood a shadowy figure. The man stepped closer to the bed, and Leo could see his thick silver hair, parted on one side. The style was familiar, forming the same wavy lines as Daddy's black hair.

"Is that any way to treat your abuelo Logroño?" he said.

Leo's heart thumped loud in the dark bedroom. "You're my abuelo? Are you from el Otro Lado?"

The man laughed. "I see they are trying to

teach you something. No, I'm still part of the living world. I came from El Paso to see you."

"Oh." Leo didn't know anything about El Paso except that it was so far away from every other Texas city, it might as well be in a different state. "Okay. Um, why?"

The man—her father's father, apparently—wore a funny dark coat that looked like the graduation gown Isabel had ordered online for her senior photos. "I came all the way here"—Abuelo Logroño paused, raising one eyebrow—"because I know about what you can do."

"What I can do?" Leo asked. "Oh, you mean magic? Yeah, we're a whole family of brujas. If you stay until morning, Mamá will tell you all about it. It's only sort of a secret."

"I'm not looking for the folk wisdom of a bruja cocinera." The way he said it, Leo's family magic sounded almost like an insult. "I came to talk about real power. The power I think you have. You're very special, Leonora Logroño."

There was something silky in his voice, and the way he smiled at Leo gave her the same warm feeling she got when Mamá trusted her with more responsibilities or when Marisol asked her opinion on an outfit. "What do you mean?" she asked, leaning forward. She wanted to know what was special about her. She wanted to earn that warm feeling.

But Abuelo Logroño shook his head, smile vanishing. "First things first. Let's see how strong you are. I would hate to find that I'm mistaken." He reached into a pocket of his long robes and dug out a handful of something pale pink and powdery. Holding his palm up to his mouth, he blew it into the air with a puff of breath.

"Call me as soon as you can," he said. "If you remember, then we'll see."

The powder sparkled in the air, bright lights dancing across Leo's vision. She covered her eyes with her hand, but it didn't help. And then everything was dark.

It had been a nightmare, hadn't it? It couldn't have been real.

With her vision ended, Leo stared into the dark corner of the office, biting her lip. Daddy never talked about his father. None of the Logroños did, not even Abuela Logroño.

But Leo's other abuela had told her—before her spirit was put to rest by Caroline's spell in January—that Daddy's family had hidden magic.

Had Leo dreamed up a mystery, or had one dropped into her lap?

"A-Abuelo?" Leo whispered into the dim office air. "Are you . . . here?"

Her voice faded, and the silence was impenetrable. She stared so hard at the darkness that her eyes started to water.

The bright tone of a bell made Leo jump like Señor Gato avoiding a puddle. The front doorbell. Leo rolled her eyes at herself, trying to summon a dream in the middle of the day.

"They're here!" Mamá's voice called. "Come say hi, girls."

Leo shook her shoulders and scampered out of the office. Trying to summon a dream relative wasn't going to make her feel any better, but her real-life relatives might.

"I'm so sorry; we're closed right now," Daddy joked, leaving the cash register to hug his sister, Leo's aunt Rita. "Come back later."

"Closed in the middle of the day?" Aunt Rita teased back. "And here I was thinking you'd finally developed some business sense, Luis."

Leo lined up behind Isabel and Marisol and Mamá to get her own crushing hug from her aunt, who smelled like flowery soap.

"My goodness," Mamá said. "JP, you've grown!"

Mamá always said that whenever she saw one of Leo's cousins, but when JP entered the bakery after his mom, Leo could see that it was true. She had last seen JP at Christmas, when he had been his normal stocky self, and since then it looked like someone had left him in a warm oven to double in size. He had outgrown Mamá already, but now he seemed to have passed Aunt Rita and was gaining on Daddy, with big hands and feet hinting at even more growth to come. He looked like he belonged on the eighth-grade football team with the cool kids, and for a minute Leo felt especially young and shy.

But then she saw him catch the front door behind him and shut it extra carefully, and he turned back into just being her cousin who Mamá had once threatened with stories of vengeful duendes who would steal his toes if he kept slamming doors. She smiled.

"Hey, Leo." JP hung back from the family bustle, avoiding hugs now that he was officially a teenager. "Happy cousins."

"Happy cousins!" Leo was pleased he'd remembered. When she was little, she had gotten so used to seeing her relatives on holidays that she had started thinking that anytime she saw her cousins was a holiday.

"Jablo Puan," Daddy delivered the silly nickname with a solemn face as he offered his hand to JP.

"Uncloo," JP responded, shaking the hand with equal fake seriousness.

"I'd better get going," Aunt Rita said, eyes flicking from her watch to JP to Daddy to her car parked in front of the curb outside. "You have all your diabetes stuff, sweetie? Pump supplies and emergency glucose tablets, and test strips, and—"

"I'm *fine*." JP shrugged his mom's hand off his shoulder. "I have everything." He patted the black fanny pack around his waist, where he kept his blood sugar meter, needles, and usually a few handfuls of candy.

"We'll take good care of him, Margarita," Mamá soothed. "And here, for the road." She held out a paper bag of orejas.

"Oh, thanks, that's so nice." Aunt Rita took the pastries, then winked. "Are they going to help me with my presentation?"

Mamá winked back. After the episode with the spirits, when Leo's friends had proved trustworthy enough to handle magical phenomena, Alma, Belén, and Leo had convinced her that they shouldn't hide their brujería from the rest of Daddy's family. Mamá agreed, and they had proudly announced their secret at Aunt Rita's birthday party in February.

But the Logroños treated it like one of Daddy's jokes, all the aunts and uncles smiling like they were playing along with a prank. Mamá hadn't helped at all, nodding and raising her eyebrows and hiding a smile behind her hand. She had known they would never believe them. She liked to keep her half secrets.

"If you need anything," Aunt Rita said, "I'm a phone call away."

"Go show those academics who deserves tenure," Daddy said with another hug.

The bell tinkled goodbye, and Aunt Rita pulled away from the curb, an oreja already stuck between her teeth.

Isabel took JP's backpack to the office and his medical supplies to the walk-in fridge, while Mamá made him choose breakfast off the bakery shelves.

"I've seen these online," JP said, reaching eagerly for a piñata cookie. "I've been wanting to try one. Did you really make them up yourself?"

Leo grinned and puffed out her chest before modestly answering, "Well, they're mostly normal puerquitos." And then she added, "But I did invent the icing."

"That's the same as a marranito, right?" JP eyed the cookie, reaching into his pocket to pull out his insulin pump and tapping buttons. "Plus extra sugar, maybe fifteen more grams? Something like that?" He dropped the pump back into his pocket and took a big bite out of his piñata's head. "Hey, that's really good! Do they have candy inside?"

"Oh, they don't, no." Leo's pride wilted slightly. "We thought about it, but—"

"They'd get all ruined in the oven, right?" JP guessed. "Or can you put them in after you make them?"

"Well, there's a way to do it with three layers of cookies with the middle cut out, but Mamá thinks—"

"So, JP," Daddy interrupted her explanation, coming up behind them to clap his nephew on the shoulder. "I'm sure you don't want to be stuck in the bakery all day talking about frosting techniques."

Leo frowned. Was she annoying her cousin? Sometimes she forgot that not everyone wanted to discuss the finer points of baking all the time (even if she did), but she didn't know why Daddy was acting like it was a totally boring topic when he knew as much about frosting techniques as anyone else in the family.

"Why don't I take you and Leo to the movies?" Daddy said. "I know Alma and Belén have been excited about the one with the dragons."

"*DragonBlood: Whispers of Dragons?*" JP's eyes lit up. "Definitely! I've been begging my mom to take me all week."

"Now that you mention it, she *might* have told me you wanted to go. . . ."

Leo's frown slowly turned into a smile. Daddy didn't really think the bakery was boring, he was just excited about the plan. Normally she wasn't allowed to see PG-13 movies, but the twins had shown her the DragonBlood books and counted down the days to the release. "Yeah, let's do it!" She was excited to have JP here, and excited for spring break, and as they drove, JP's contagious excitement made her even more excited for the dragons.

Still, in the dark of the movie theater, she caught herself checking the corners for hidden figures, and at least once she could have sworn that she saw a pair of laughing eyes peering back at her.

That night, Leo tossed beneath her orange comforter. Every time she started to doze, sparkling pink lights danced against her eyelids, and it was getting *annoying*. Sitting up, she rubbed her eyes until they watered.

Señor Gato was locked in her room for the night so he wouldn't sneak into Alma and Belén's room,

where JP was sleeping, and start his allergies acting up. Leo wasn't allergic to cat dander, but she
felt like something was irritating her eyelids and
tickling the back of her throat.

"Is this your fault?" Leo asked the black cat,
whose bright green eyes blinked at her from the foot
of her bed. Then she glanced at the corner of the
room. "Or is it . . . something else?" She had spent
most of the day convincing herself that the dream
hadn't been real, but the darkness made it all seem
suddenly possible. "Is . . . is somebody there?"

Señor Gato turned his stare on the corner. The
hair on Leo's arms prickled up in goose bumps and
something like a voice in her head whispered, "Not
good enough."

Leo's breath caught. "Abuelo," she said, as clearly
as she could in a whisper. "Abuelo Logroño."

Because she was watching for it, this time she
noticed the tiny shimmer in the air as Abuelo
Logroño stepped out of nothing and into her bedroom.

"Well done, young Logroño," he said softly. "Very
well done."

Instead of feeling proud, or relieved that she
hadn't been so out of sorts over nothing more than a
dream, Leo felt mad. She yanked the chain to turn

on her bedside table lamp, making Abuelo Logroño wince at the sudden brightness.

"What did you do to me?" she demanded. "It won't let me sleep."

Señor Gato padded up the bed to stand beside her, tail puffed and ears folded back, protecting her. Leo made a mental note to feed him treats in the morning.

Her grandfather waved his hand, and Leo flinched, thinking he was throwing more sparkly powder at her. He was dressed in the same black robes with sleeves that puffed wide around his hands. "Settle down," he said, "It's only a simple illusion spell. You were able to see through it easily enough, so removing it shouldn't be a problem."

"But I don't know how to remove it," Leo whined. "It's your spell."

Abuelo Logroño raised his eyebrows. "You can't remove an illusion spell? Someone has neglected your education. A young brujo should learn to defend himself."

"Herself," Leo corrected. "I'm a bruja."

"I was speaking of the principle." Abuelo Logroño waved a hand, sleeve flapping. "But that's all the more reason for your teachers to make sure you aren't left vulnerable to attack."

The lights still winked at the corners of Leo's eyes, making it hard to focus. "Why would anybody want to attack me?"

"That's one of the things I wanted to talk to you about, now that you've proven your talent." With another wave of his hand, Abuelo Logroño created a fluffy white cloud that floated over and engulfed Leo's head. It felt a little like spiderwebs tickling her skin and eyelashes, but when the cloud dispersed, the lights and the restless feeling from the day were gone. Leo breathed a sigh of relief.

"Well?" Abuelo Logroño said. "Aren't you going to say thank you?"

Leo absolutely was not going to thank someone for fixing a problem he had caused in the first place. She crossed her arms over her chest. "How do you keep appearing in my room?"

A smile crept onto the old man's face. "That, young Logroño, is the other thing I'm here to tell you about."

CHAPTER 5
LOGROÑO MAGIC

Abuelo Logroño clapped his hands, and the air around Leo's bedroom rippled. "That's better," he said, speaking in a loud voice instead of a whisper, "A silencing spell will make sure we're not overheard."

"How did you . . . ?" Leo began. "You can cast spells, just like that?"

Abuelo Logroño laughed. "I can do a lot more than that, young Logroño, and so can you. You see, you are heir to a very old line of magic."

"I know," Leo said. "My great-great-great-great-great-grandmother was the first bruja in our family to open a bakery, and—"

"No, no." Abuelo Logroño looked like an oversized crow flapping his wings in annoyance. "Not your mother's family. The Logroño legacy stretches back so much farther, long before our ancestors came across the Atlantic as explorers in a new world."

Leo frowned. "Ms. Wood—that's my teacher—said we shouldn't call it a 'new world' when there were already people living on it."

Her abuelo made the wing-flapping motion again. He sort of looked like he was swatting away her words like flies. "We have been a powerful brujo family for countless generations. Your great-grandmother on your mother's side was . . . creative, anchoring her magic the way she did. Maybe in a few hundred years, her magical legacy will grow strong enough . . . but it's such an odd case, and so unstable. Likely it won't last long enough to find out."

Leo was feeling a lot better without the illusion spell hanging over her head, but this was still the second night in a row of interrupted sleep, and she wasn't at all sure she liked the way Abuelo Logroño talked about her family magic, or the way he talked at all—speaking at Leo, instead of listening to her.

"Are you getting to the point?" she grumbled. "Why did you come here? What do you think I can do?"

Abuelo Logroño ruffled the sides of his robe as he stepped toward Leo's bed. His eyes crinkled with excitement the way Daddy's did when they'd come out of the dragon movie, or the way Isabel's did when she researched a new magical theory.

"You carry the powers of the Logroño legacy, the first in two generations. We have powerful brujería, the kind that obscures what we don't wish to reveal. We can bend what others see, sense, or remember. And most powerful of all, we have the ability to touch the shadows between worlds."

Leo didn't understand every word in that speech, but the last part at least sounded familiar. "Are you talking about the veil?" she asked. "I already learned how to do that in January. I had to help pull a bunch of spirits out of the living world and back into el Otro Lado." Leo didn't quite trust her visitor enough to tell him about Caroline's magic, so she didn't. "Ever since then, I can see the veil sometimes, and even touch it. Well, my fingers go through."

As she spoke, Abuelo Logroño's smile widened and the creases around his eyes deepened. Leo felt that same warm pride color her cheeks, and soon her smile matched his.

Mamá and Tía Paloma had made Leo sit down and talk with them after she had jumped through the veil to save the spirits. They said she should be careful with unknown magic, and that she had acted rashly. Because they were so worried about the "potential consequences" of Leo interacting with the veil, she hadn't exactly gotten around to telling them how she could sometimes see and reach for it. But now, with her abuelo smiling at her, she found she almost felt excited to share the secret.

"Amazing," Abuelo Logroño said. "Absolutely improbable. Such great power, with no training at all. You must have a natural ability stronger than we've seen in a hundred years."

"I have been training," Leo reminded him, but it was hard to stay annoyed in the face of such glowing compliments. "Do you really think I have great power?"

"I do. And I was talking about *real* training, in your Logroño powers." Abuelo Logroño clapped his hands together, making Señor Gato startle and jump off the bed, flicking his tail at Leo as he went. "That settles it," the old brujo said. "You must start training with me immediately."

"What?" Leo said.

"You're already quite far behind, and raw power can't make up for that. But I hope you won't give up. Logroños don't shrink from a task just because it's challenging."

This conversation felt like a mixer turned on too fast, with puffs of flour flying in every direction. "Of course I won't give up," she said. "But—"

Abuelo Logroño nodded before she could go on. "Excellent. I'm counting on you to keep that promise."

Leo wasn't sure she had made any promise. "I . . . I need some time to think about all this," she said. "I mean, I'm already in the middle of magic training."

"Think about it?" Abuelo Logroño ran his hand through his gray hair, looking so much like Daddy for a second that Leo felt guilty disappointing him. "Young Logroño, there are forces at work here you can't begin to understand." He sat down on the edge of the bed, collapsing as if a weight had fallen on him. "The old traditions are weakening, dying. Not a single one of my children carries my power. Everywhere, brujos who fight the good fight are becoming less common—and less powerful."

Despite her misgivings, Leo felt bad for the sad old man. "Fight?" she asked. "What fight?"

"The fight against supernatural beings!" Abuelo Logroño practically shouted. "Surely you know that humanity is not the only intelligent and magical species to share space on this earth."

Leo shrugged her shoulders up to her ears. She knew about ghosts and spirits, but she didn't think they counted as not human. A flash of the movie she'd seen earlier flickered in her brain. "Like dragons?"

"Dragons?" He scoffed. "Those glorified grass snakes are the least of our worries. Animal control is for lesser brujos, or any nonmagical youth with a big enough stick."

Leo racked her brains for any mention of dangerous magical creatures. Of course she'd heard legends of duendes, Bloody Mary, el chupacabras—scary stories Marisol told to keep her up at night. But Mamá and Tía Paloma had never mentioned any of those in her magic lessons. Abuela had talked about La Llorona once, but she was just a ghost who'd had the bad luck of getting stuck with unfinished business on the wrong side of the veil.

Leo remembered that when she'd needed to help trapped spirits cross the veil in January, they almost hadn't made it. Spells to cross between worlds didn't work without a guide, and guides were dangerous nonhuman creatures. Tía Paloma had forbidden Caroline and Isabel to mess with any of the spells that told them how to summon those guides, even though they risked keeping the spirits trapped and suffering. Luckily, Leo had been able to act as a guide herself using her birth-order magic.

"Is it like . . ." Leo didn't know the name of the creatures Tía Paloma was so afraid of. "Like the guides that you can summon to cross through the veil?"

Abuelo Logroño nodded. "Evil specters," he said. "Creatures that never knew life. Very tricky to control if you do summon them, but I can teach you how. And they're not the only ones. Sirens, and bloodsuckers, and shape-shifters of all kinds. Goblins and elves and a million more species of hidden parasites. The world needs your power, and you need me to train you for the things you'll face. You were impressed by my spell casting, but you, mija, will be able to do more than cast simple spells. I believe you have the capacity to master the most difficult of the Logroño powers—to become a saltasombras, like me."

"Salta . . . sombras?" Leo broke the Spanish word apart to try to understand it. "Jump and shadow?"

Abuelo Logroño stood up, his dark robes swirling around him. "A saltasombras. He who jumps through shadows—though, taking a few grammatical liberties, 'shadow hopper' might be a better translation."

SHE who jumps through shadows, Leo thought stubbornly.

"The shadow between worlds, what you call the

veil? We have the power to move through it at will. You can hide yourself and your movements. Or at least, you might someday. If you train with me." He smoothed down his hair, which he had ruffled in his enthusiasm. "Think about it, young Logroño. When you're ready to begin, call me, just as you did tonight."

"My name is Leo—"

In a shimmer of darkness, Abuelo Logroño was gone.

Leo pulled the covers up to her chin and stared for a long time at the shadows into which her grandfather had melted.

CHAPTER 6
THE TRUTH

Leo watched the wind shake the branches outside her window, the shadows of the leaves shifting across her desk in the early-morning light. Everything about the magical visitor replayed in her head, as confusing and thrilling and annoying as it had been when it happened. All night she had drifted between restless worry and restless excitement, her dream self hopscotching through dark puddles, splashing Mamá's and Tía Paloma's white aprons as they followed her.

Abuelo Logroño promised powerful magic, but Leo didn't like the way he talked about her mother's family.

Sleep had disappeared for good this time, so Leo sat up. It was too early even for Mamá to be awake, but her alarm would go off soon now. Leo wasn't scheduled to open the bakery today, but with Tía Paloma and the twins gone, Mamá probably wouldn't turn away an extra pair of hands. Leo kicked off her covers and stood, checking all four shadowy corners of her room before moving to her closet to pick out shorts and a T-shirt for the day.

She brushed her hair and teeth in the dark, turning the bathroom sink on to just a soft drip. The house was never this still, and it made Leo shiver. She snuck down the hallway, past Alma and Belén's room where JP softly snored, past Señor Gato, who eyed her suspiciously before returning to grooming himself. In the kitchen she checked the clock again . . . 4:05. Just under half an hour until Mamá would rise.

The streetlamp shining through the blinds made streaks of light and shadow on the counter. Leo waved her hands through the pattern, watching them change colors. If she went fast enough, the rippling effect made her fingers look like they were shimmering. Or maybe . . . Leo stopped moving to check whether her eyes were playing tricks on her. The shadows didn't look unusual, but when she dipped her fingers in, she thought she saw a shimmering ripple.

Someone who jumps through shadows, who can appear and disappear in an instant . . . a saltasombras. Leo set two fingers on the countertop to make her hand into a person, standing on two finger legs, and hopped them into a line of shadow.

She let out a squeak when the tips of both fingers vanished into thin air.

When she had managed to do that before, she had thought she was reaching into el Otro Lado, stepping through a gate like the one she had used to take the spirits home. She wasn't even sure she wanted to practice doing *that*. But Abuelo Logroño had said that one day she might be able to hide in shadow.

She *did* have the power her abuelo described. With the right training, could her whole body jump in and out of shadows that easily?

If she did that, could she still be a bruja cocinera like her mother, aunt, and sisters? Or would she have to leave her bakery training behind?

Leo's fingers came back into sight slowly, tingling at the edges like they had fallen asleep. She didn't know what to think or feel, so she stood up and wandered to the refrigerator. There was plenty of milk and a whole carton of eggs, but the cereal boxes above the fridge were all down to the very last crumbs except for Daddy's fiber crunch, and Leo still didn't know how to cook anything on the stove. But she knew how to use the oven.

Leo didn't know what she should do, how she wanted to answer Abuelo Logroño's offer, or why she had this ability to disappear into the shadows, but she was still a bakery bruja in training, and she knew how to keep herself busy in a kitchen.

"Leo, what's all this?" Mamá came into the room just as Leo popped the biscuits into the oven.

"I couldn't sleep," Leo explained. "I thought you might like to eat breakfast before work."

"But that's . . ." Mamá watched Leo rinse mixing bowls and measuring cups in the sink. "Oh, 'jita," she sighed.

Leo stiffened. "What's wrong?"

"Nothing, nothing," Mamá helped Leo wipe down the counter and hugged her around one shoulder. Leo thought she heard her sniff. "It's just that one minute I'm watching to make sure you don't crawl too close to the hot oven, and the next minute you're old enough to use it to bake surprise breakfast biscuits. . . ."

"Mamá," she whined, shrugging out of the hug, "I've been using the oven for months."

"I know." Mamá sat down at the kitchen table, smiling at Leo with suspiciously watery eyes. "I forget sometimes how much you've grown since last November, that's all."

Last November Leo hadn't known as much about baking, and she hadn't known anything at all about magic. She had been sneaky about what she learned, keeping secrets from her family and trying to learn magic without letting them find out.

She had grown since then.

"Mamá, I need to tell you something."

Mamá raised her eyebrows. "Oh no. These aren't bribery biscuits are they? What did you do?"

"No, it's not that." Leo said quickly. "I had a . . . um . . . visitor. In the middle of the night. It was . . . Abuelo Logroño."

Mamá's teasing smile disappeared, and she straightened in her chair. She stayed still and quiet long enough that Leo almost repeated herself, but she was afraid of making Mamá angrier.

"Visited from el Otro Lado, you mean?" Mamá finally asked. "He's crossed over to the other side of the veil?" If she was sad about the idea that Abuelo Logroño might have passed on, she didn't show it; her tone was flat and serious.

Leo shook her head. "Alive. He wanted to talk about my magic."

Mamá's hand slammed against the kitchen table, making Leo jump.

"That old vulture," she muttered. "I told Paloma that a blood curse would last longer, but she was so sure he'd lose interest. Luis!" Mamá sprang to her feet, wrapping her bathrobe more tightly around her before pulling Leo against her side and shepherding her out of the kitchen and down the hall. "Luis! Wake up!"

Isabel poked her head out of the bathroom, a toothbrush hanging out of her half-open mouth. An annoyed grumble floating out of the older girls' bedroom meant that Marisol was also awake.

"Luis!" Mamá pulled Leo into her and Daddy's bedroom and slammed the door behind her. Daddy sat on the edge of the bed, reading one of Alma and Belén's comics he had promised to finish before they got back from the convention.

"Elena?" he asked, voice still a little deep with sleepiness. "Leo? Is everything okay?"

Mamá took one deep breath—the kind she always tried to teach Marisol to take before saying something she might regret. "Álvaro came into Leo's room last night," she said, her voice quiet and sharp. "Apparently he had something to say about magic."

Daddy's face scrunched like he was smelling a rotten egg, or watching the news. He slowly closed the comic. "How did he get in?" he asked, eyes on the book as he laid it carefully on the bedside table.

"¿Con fe y esfuerzo?" Mamá sighed. "How should I know? He might have come through the front door, because clearly the wards are failing. I don't even know if it's sabotage or normal wear and tear; it's been years now."

"Almost fifteen." Daddy ran a hand through his hair. "I'm so sorry," he said. "I thought we had put a stop to this nonsense."

"What nonsense?" Leo was more confused than ever. Nothing about her parents' reaction was what she'd expected. She had thought the hardest part to explain would have been—

"Wait, you knew?" she asked Daddy. "That Abuelo Logroño had magic?"

Daddy dropped his head and cleared his throat.

"But . . . you lied!" She gulped and tried to quiet her loud voice and louder pulse before she continued. "You said your family didn't have any . . . you said that—" A terrible idea entered her head. "Are you a brujo too? Were you ever going to tell me?"

"Leo." Daddy jumped off the bed and tried to wrap her in a hug, but he held up his hands and stepped back when she flinched away. Instead, he knelt on the floor in front of her, eyes level with hers. "I'm not a brujo," he said. "Everything I told you was the truth: I don't have powers, my family doesn't have powers." Leo scowled and scoffed, but Daddy shook his head. "My father . . . wasn't part of my life. He left as soon as he realized that none of his children—me, your aunt Rita, your uncle Alberto—had any magic."

Leo frowned at the ground. Now she remembered Abuelo Logroño saying that his children had no powers. When she'd first found out that all her sisters were practicing magic without her, she had worried that her own powers didn't exist. She had spent months wondering why she didn't have a birth-order power. And even after leading the spirits through the gate in January, she had worried that her power wasn't nearly as strong or useful as the rest of her family's abilities. But as much as she hated the thought of being left out of the bakery secrets, she had never worried that her family wouldn't love her if she didn't have magic.

Poor Daddy.

"Your grandma never told us much besides his name. I grew up totally unmagical in a totally unmagical family. Everything I told you—about meeting your mamá, about not believing the things she told me—all that is true."

Leo started to feel guilty for accusing Daddy of lying, but then he continued.

"It wasn't until Isabel was born that Álvaro showed up. I had never known him, but suddenly here he was, making a lot of fancy speeches about her birthright. I guess he expected us to be dazzled by the idea of magic, or if that wasn't enough, then by his illusion spell." Daddy's frown turned into a crooked smile. "He definitely didn't count on Elena and Lucero having powers of their own."

Leo smiled too, imagining Mamá and Abuela facing off against the old brujo. In her head, the two sides of her family posed on either side of a jagged red line like the characters on the cover of Alma and Belén's comic, except instead of fighting over treasure or the fate of the world, they were fighting over a baby.

"He wanted to test Isabel's power and train her in the Logroño style," Mamá said. "We tried to explain that we had our own way of doing things as brujas cocineras. We were never interested in our children's following Álvaro's path."

Leo wasn't sure why there had to be two paths. "Because he can make himself invisible?" she asked. She thought of the way her own fingers had disappeared into the shadows; she hid her hands behind her back.

"Of course not," Mamá said. "This isn't about what power he has. It's . . . Just trust me, Leo, he's bad news."

"Well, it sounds like maybe he just wanted to teach us different magic." Leo raised her chin while Mamá and Daddy frowned at each other. "That doesn't seem like a bad thing."

"It's not an issue of different powers," Mamá said. "It's an issue of different philosophy. What he thinks power is for."

"He told me it was to protect people," Leo said. "To protect humans from . . . I don't know, monsters and things. Vampires and . . . what are sirens?"

"Sirenas are mermaids," Daddy said softly. Leo's eyes popped open. Mermaids were real? And Abuelo Logroño wanted to fight them?

"He called them monsters." Mamá clicked her tongue. "They're just magical folk, same as brujos and brujas."

"But mermaids," Leo whispered reverently.

"Magical humans like us, we recognize and respect that we aren't the only intelligent species sharing this world," Mamá fumed. "We don't go bothering nature spirits or hadas that aren't hurting anyone. Your grandfather is part of an old tradition and an old war that the rest of us stopped fighting centuries ago. Magical communities can govern themselves and have been doing it for years. Some of them want to live hidden among nonmagical folks, but most keep to themselves. The only conflict comes from folks like him who don't want to let old prejudices die." Mamá's chest rose and fell, her face pink. "I'm sorry, Leo, I'm not angry at you. It just makes me so . . ." She huffed out a long breath. "I've raised this question with the Southwest Regional Brujería and Spellcraft Association before—they should be doing more to stop Álvaro and his type, watching him more closely. His ideas are dangerous. I was raised to use magic for love, and that's what I want to teach my girls."

"You did. I just didn't know anything about magical communities or . . . I didn't know."

Leo wanted to use magic the way Mamá did, to make people happy and bring people together. She didn't want to hurt anyone, magical or not. She kind of wanted to meet a mermaid. But when Abuelo Logroño had told her she could fight for good, it had felt more exciting and heroic than baking lucky cookies. It felt like something that would happen in a movie Daddy would want to see, not something he would think was boring.

Abuelo Logroño had lied about magical folk,

calling them dangerous monsters. Mamá had lied about them too, by not telling Leo they existed. She and Daddy had both lied about his family magic. When would grown-ups stop lying about everything important?

"I got sloppy," Mamá said. "Álvaro would show up when each of you girls were born, getting more and more insistent until we finally decided to keep him away with warding spells. That was when Alma and Belén were little, and we haven't seen him since. I assumed he had given up by now; it's been years since I renewed the spell." Mamá sighed. "It couldn't have happened at a worse time, with Easter orders coming in for next week, and us so shorthanded."

"I can handle a warding spell." Isabel spoke from the doorway, startling Leo and both her parents. Marisol leaned over her shoulder, waving sheepishly. "I'm sorry," Isabel added, pulling the door shut behind them. "But you were kind of . . . yelling. We came to warn you to keep it down so you wouldn't wake up JP. And then, well, we couldn't help overhearing. I've been reading about wards. You and I can do this, Mamá."

"I suppose," Mamá said. "But then we won't be able to open the bakery today."

"Why not?" Marisol asked. "If it's that important, Leo and I can handle it, with Daddy's help. We might not get all the shelves full, but we can still stay open as long as we have bolillos and conchas."

"And we wouldn't have to be gone for the whole day just to cast a warding spell," Isabel added. "We can be back before lunch probably."

Mamá chewed her lip. "You girls are right." She scrunched her eyebrows at Leo. "Let Marisol start up the oven and swap the trays, okay, 'jita? Luis, you can help with that part. Use oven mitts this time, please." Daddy looked offended by the advice, but Mamá ignored him. "We'll get this done as soon as we can, and then we'll be back at the bakery before you— Oh!" Mamá's arms flew up in frustration. "But what about JP?"

"Don't worry," Leo said. "I have an idea for him. Can I borrow someone's phone?"

Marisol tucked her phone back into her pocket slowly, but Isabel passed hers over.

"I have to ask . . . do we really need to do all this?" Marisol said. "You're sure we can't just, I don't know, talk to the guy? If he's our abuelo?"

Isabel frowned and elbowed her sister while Leo punched in the memorized numbers and sent her text. "But when else will I ever get a chance to do a warding spell?" she whispered.

Daddy put one hand on Marisol's shoulder. "My

father," he said, "is not someone we want you girls to have in your lives. It's not just that he cares about power more than anything, or has a pattern of ignoring us when we try to talk to him. He knows how to manipulate people."

Leo thought about how proud she had felt when Abuelo Logroño had told her she had power greater than anyone else in her family. He'd made it seem special. But . . . there was also a hint of cruelty to his compliments.

"We should do it," she said. Isabel's phone buzzed in her hand, and she smiled reading the response. "Let's get going. I have biscuits for breakfast, and Caroline's going to meet us at the bakery to babysit JP in like an hour."

Leo felt a twinge of disappointment letting go of the idea of becoming a powerful hero, the only person strong enough to stand in the face of danger. But that idea sounded lonely anyway. She'd much rather face danger with the power of her family surrounding her.

CHAPTER 7
HONEYBEES

The front doorbell dinged just as Leo handed JP a stack of dirty bowls to carry to the sink. Her cousin, who was unaccustomed to bakers' hours and was half asleep on his feet, had insisted on helping, since Mamá and Isabel had to stay home to handle the "pest problem" Leo claimed to have discovered in the middle of the night. It was nice of him to want to help, Leo had reminded herself at least twenty times while shooing JP away from tasting raw cookie dough or burning himself on a hot cake tin. Still, she rushed out of the kitchen at the sound of the bell, excited to greet Caroline and Brent, both of them still wiping sleep from their eyes.

"Hi, Mr. Logroño." Brent yawned hugely, his eyes glued to the bakery shelves. "May I please have something to eat?"

Leo had promised Brent free bakery food for life after his help rounding up the pack of spirits in January, but Daddy hated to see the perpetually hungry sixth grader raiding the shelves, so Brent made a point to ask permission.

"Help yourself." Daddy smiled, "You too, Caroline. I hope Leo didn't wake you up too early."

"There aren't any cinnamon rolls yet," Leo said, guessing what Caroline was looking for on the still half-empty shelves. "Thanks for coming, both of you. It's just me and Marisol this morning, so we're a little bit behind."

Brent widened his eyes over a huge mouthful of pineapple empanada. "Wha'appened?"

The saloon-style blue doors between the bakery kitchen and storefront clacked open and Marisol appeared, ushering JP out ahead of her and looking frazzled.

"Just a pest problem at home," she said, wiping a line of flour off her cheek but leaving a streak of chocolate in its place. "Mamá and Isabel are dealing with it."

"Couldn't y'all call an exterminator?" Brent asked. Caroline, seeing Leo's tiny head shake, tried to quiet him by tugging his sleeve, but he was busy taking another bite and eyeing JP curiously. "Who's this?"

"That's probably her cousin," Caroline whispered. "The one we're going to hang out with?"

"You're Leo's cousin?" Brent's mouth hung open, braces flashing, "But you're so tall!"

JP nodded and waved. Leo hoped introductions might work to change the subject, but instead JP said, "I was wondering why there wasn't an exterminator around too. I figured it was because this is such a small town. Like how y'all don't have food delivery apps."

Caroline let out a surprised laugh.

"Actually, Brent," Leo said sharply, "it's something my mom wants to take care of herself because it's kind of *special* and delicate. I think she has an old family *tradition* to deal with pests."

"That's a weird family traditi— Oh," Brent's eyes lit up just in time to avoid getting his toes stomped by Leo in a desperate attempt to clue him in. "Um, yep, that makes sense. We're just, uh, small-town folk who like to take care of pests ourselves. Like, uh, farmers." Caroline raised her eyebrows, and Brent shrugged.

"Anyway, hi." Caroline smiled wide at JP. "We're Leo's friends. We're not farmers. I used to live in Houston. You live in Austin, right?"

"Yeah, but I was in Houston for a while too," JP said, and smiled. He left Marisol's side to get closer to Leo and her friends.

"Cool!" Caroline squeaked. "Um, at least I hope it was cool. I hope you weren't there to go to the medical center, like my family." The tips of her ears were bright pink, which wasn't totally unusual, but her shyness usually made her quiet, not squeaky and talkative.

"I'm Brent." Brent held out his hand; JP hesitated before shaking it. "I don't live in Houston."

"Yeah, I figured you lived here," JP said. He glanced at Leo, who couldn't offer any explanation for why her friends were babbling. "I'm JP."

Caroline and Brent both laughed at that for some reason. JP was right about Rose Hill being small. New faces always created a stir of excitement, but it was funny to think of JP like a mysterious new kid in school.

A customer came in, sending Marisol scurrying back into the kitchen and Daddy back to his seat at the cash register. Leo wanted to help, but she also wanted to make sure her friends weren't going to scare her cousin when they were supposed to be entertaining him.

"Your fanny pack looks useful," Brent blurted. "And I like your T-shirt."

JP's brow had furrowed during the conversation, but it smoothed into a smile when he looked down at the complimented shirt, which sported a dragon on the front.

"Have you seen *DragonBlood* yet?"

"Keep up your guard, friend of dragons." Brent quoted the movie with his arm crossed over his chest like the dragon queen, hopping excitedly on his toes. "I'm kind of a huge fan. I've seen it three times so far."

"I've read all the books," Caroline announced, her face pink all over now.

"Yeah, but you weren't even going to see the movie until I dragged you," Brent muttered. Caroline's mouth twisted in annoyance.

Marisol reentered the front of the bakery with a tray balanced on each arm, and Leo rushed to help her before she spilled bolillos all over the floor. "Are your friends okay?" Marisol whispered. "They look like they've never seen an out-of-towner before."

Leo nodded, emptying her tray into the clear bolillo bin and stacking it on top of Marisol's. Soon Brent and Caroline would realize JP was just her dragon-loving older cousin and stop gawking.

In the meantime, she took advantage of their interest, following Marisol back into the chaos of the kitchen. When she returned to shelve a tray of cinnamon rolls, JP and Caroline were talking excitedly about a Houston taco chain, and Brent was sulking, though he perked up at the sight of Leo's warm treats.

"I happen to think there are plenty of great local restaurants right here in Rose Hill," Daddy pointed out, giving Leo a wink from the front counter.

"Are there?" JP asked. "I've only really eaten stuff from the bakery." He realized his mistake when Daddy dropped his jaw in mock outrage, and he scrambled to backtrack by saying that of course nothing in Austin or Houston could compare with Amor y Azúcar.

"We have other good places too," Brent said, worming his way between Caroline and JP. "The Flores's place has the best enchiladas, and there are spicy noodles at the gas station,"

"Pho," Caroline corrected.

"And Honeybees!" Brent added triumphantly.

"Honeybees?" Leo asked. "Is that the new place? Is it a restaurant?"

"Yeah, you haven't seen the signs?" Caroline asked. "They're advertising all along Main street. *Opening Soon: Honeybees Café and Sweet Treats.*"

"Hmm . . ." Daddy leaned over the counter. "I

hadn't seen those, no. I wonder why the owner didn't run that past the business association first."

"How come?" Leo asked.

"Well, we already have a dessert bakery in town." Daddy said. "Stores in town try to avoid competing with each other—it's better for everyone that way." His smile didn't quite cancel out the worry lines between his eyebrows.

"Is it bad to have more than one bakery?" Caroline asked. "Houston has lots of the same types of restaurants."

"But Rose Hill doesn't have as many hungry people," JP said. "So every person counts. And anyone who buys a cookie from Honeybees isn't buying one from here."

"But who would want to buy a cookie from some new store instead of an Amor y Azúcar cookie?" Leo demanded.

"Excellent point." Daddy nodded. "I sure wouldn't want to go up against this beloved town institution." He patted the old cash register. "Excuse me, ladies and gents." He hopped off his stool and headed into the kitchen, pulling his phone out as he went.

Leo bit her lip. Daddy whistled behind the blue doors, but Leo wasn't fooled by the cheery tune. His eyes were still worried about the competition of another Rose Hill bakery. She would bet he was going to call Mamá.

Leo looked at the half-bare shelves, the empty register. "I'd better get back to work," she said.

"Sorry for bringing bad news." Caroline twirled her butterfly ring around her finger nervously.

"I can stay and help," JP offered. "I want to learn how to use the big mixer."

"Oh no." Brent's face fell. "We were going to take you to the library while Leo works."

Caroline tapped the backpack hanging low and full over her shoulders. "I brought books to return, so if you want to check anything out, you can use my card."

"And there's a room just full of board games, plus a big graphic-novel section." Brent bounced in excitement. "We can play Catan."

JP looked at Leo, who breathed a silent sigh of relief as she waved encouragingly. "You should go," she said, reminding herself to bake something special for Caroline and Brent to thank them for such a perfect idea. "We'll be fine. I'll join y'all at the library just as soon as my mom gets back. The mixer will still be here tomorrow." And it would be safer without her cousin messing around with it while she tried to work.

"You can ride on the back of my bike," Brent offered, his face as pink as Caroline's.

Caroline hung back as the boys left to unlock the bikes. "Leo, one thing," she said, shrugging the straps of her backpack off and letting it thump onto the tiled floor. "I made something. For your mom, to thank her and Paloma for helping me with my magic lessons." Caroline dug through the bag as she talked, stopping to stack a few thick library books on the floor with care. She pulled out a foil-wrapped bundle, peeling back the silver to reveal the tip of a green candle. "It's for good luck in finances, buying and selling, that sort of thing," Caroline explained. "Maybe it will turn out to be useful for this Honeybees problem."

Leo accepted the candle with a nod, grateful that Caroline hadn't fallen for her dad's lies about everything being just fine either. "Caroline, I wanted to tell you. The pest problem—"

"Is really a magical problem?" Caroline smiled. "I got that."

Leo smiled. "But it's complicated. My abuelo from my dad's side of the family who I didn't know was alive showed up, and he tried to get me to leave with him and let him train me in powerful but sort of evil magic. My mom's trying to make sure he can't come back."

"Wow." Caroline's eyes widened. "Wait, what? Wait, your dad's family doesn't have magic, do they?"

"Apparently!" Leo threw her hands up. "I'm confused too." She wanted to say more, but Brent knocked on the bakery window and waved for Caroline to hurry.

"Tell me more later?" Caroline said. "It sounds scary and confusing. I'll make another candle. Good luck."

"Thanks. And thanks for watching JP; I'm sorry we couldn't all hang out like I wanted to."

"Oh, it's no problem at all." Caroline ducked to hide her eyes behind her bangs and twirled her ring. "He seems really nice. And cool. And Ihavetogonow, bye!" She stuffed her books into her backpack and darted out the door with only one strap over her arm.

Leo shook her head. What was happening? JP was just . . . JP.

She sniffed the candle, trying to identify the herb scent in the wax. If she weren't so busy, she could use the molcajete to infuse all the bakery ingredients with herbs to boost prosperity. Of course, Mamá warned about using luck and money spells too often, especially strong ones. Their effects started to weaken when overused, and that could leave a person vulnerable to mal de ojo. Caroline's candle was a good compromise: subtle like most of her family's magic, just enough to give things a nudge in the right direction.

Leo set the candle next to the cash register and hustled back into the kitchen, where Marisol was growling about doing all the work around here.

CHAPTER 8
DOWNRIGHT SNOOPING

Mamá and Isabel came in just before lunch, smelling like herbs and smoke and spicy-sweet magic.

"That was so cool," Isabel gushed. Marisol was doing her best to ignore her sister while she lined up trays in front of the oven, but Isabel didn't notice. "It's a lot like a summoning spell, which you'll remember we worked with when we were conjuring portals for the spirits, but we mixed it with baking brujería, because we absolutely want to play to our strengths for this kind of spell—"

Marisol slammed the oven door shut, and the clang made Isabel jump. Leo shook her head at her middle sister. Marisol would never have wanted to stay home and work strange spells with Mamá, so why was she upset at being left to work in the bakery?

"I'm so curious as to why Mamá's warding spell wore off," Isabel went on, leaning against the counter and staring at the ceiling. "I know there are some spells that weaken over time and others that grow stronger the longer they last. . . . There's so much to learn." She sighed dreamily. "I can't wait to study more."

Leo smiled, pulling herself onto a stool to take a needed break from preparing dough. She knew exactly how her older sister felt.

"I don't know how much deep magic theory you think you're going to be studying in the near future," Marisol huffed, "but I don't think your college is going to be holding magic lessons. Once you move in, you'll be way too busy with school to keep training and researching magic."

"You don't know what you're talking about," Isabel huffed right back, losing her dreamy stare to glare at her sister.

"I know that you're going to leave, and the rest of us will be stuck here picking up your slack at the bakery," Marisol muttered.

"Well, maybe there wouldn't be so much slack to pick up if you weren't always trying to do as little work as possible!"

Isabel's temper didn't usually flare so quickly, even with Marisol, but her puffed-out chest and stubbornly set mouth meant she was ready for a fight. Leo, deciding it was better not to get caught in one of her sisters' squabbles, backed away from the kitchen workspace and headed for the back hall. It was time for her break anyway.

". . . as good as Paloma and I could have done, maybe even better. It should hold fine as long as— Luis, are you even listening?"

Leo paused outside the office as Mamá talked and Daddy hummed distractedly while he tapped keys on his computer. She didn't want to walk from one fight straight into another one.

"Sorry," Daddy said, probably in response to a Mamá glare. "I'm glad Isabel did so well. That's one less thing to worry about."

"What's wrong?" Mamá asked. "Was everything okay with the girls? JP?"

Leo pressed her back against the wall so that the half-open door hid her from sight. She was crossing a line from accidental eavesdropping to downright snooping, but if Daddy wouldn't tell the truth of his worries to the whole family, then what choice did she have?

"I'm not sure yet . . . can you take a look at this email?"

Mamá sighed softly. "Why does this landlord write like he swallowed all his fancy law-school teachers?"

"They're talking about increasing the rent," Daddy said. "Look at this."

Mamá sighed again, louder. "Well, that's . . . I guess the new house will have to wait after all."

Leo's heart sank. Mamá had wanted a new house for so long.

"The increase is exactly how much you and I had budgeted for mortgage payments on the new place," Daddy said. "*Exactly*. Does that seem fishy to you?"

"Like, a curse, or a hex?" Mamá asked. "I don't know. . . . We knew a new landlord could mean changes. What would your father—or anyone— stand to gain from disappointing us?"

Leo tried to imagine someone—a fancy landlord or her not-so-nice abuelo or *anyone*—being mad enough to hurt her family. The idea scrunched up her face and her intestines and made her want to melt into the wall, or maybe punch it.

"That's not the only thing," Daddy was saying. "Have you heard about this new place, Honeybees?"

Leo listened to Daddy explain his fears, how a new bakery opening would hurt Amor y Azúcar's business. How that, combined with the new rent, combined with Isabel's college tuition, might mean worse than just not buying a new house. Leo couldn't put Daddy's desperate words together with the happy face he'd shown to her and her friends earlier.

"You're catastrophizing, Luis," Mamá said. "We can try negotiating with the landlord. And are we sure this Honeybees is even a bakery?"

The clacking of the keyboard echoed through the hall, fast as a racing heartbeat.

"'Coming soon,'" Mamá read in a whisper. "'Organic fair-trade tea and locally sourced raw honey . . . there, bakery, click where it says bakery . . . an upscale take on classic Texas favorites . . . the highest-quality ingredients make up our brioche-like pan dulces and palmiers—' They're called orejas! This is our menu. They're stealing our menu!"

"Shh," Daddy warned. "The girls will hear. So it's not just a bakery, it's a panadería. Perfect."

"An upscale panadería." Mamá's voice lowered in volume but not intensity. "Amor y Azúcar has fed this town for generations—we don't need an upscale replacement!"

"I know that, and the town knows that," Daddy soothed.

"And what are these: clove and hibiscus conchas?

What trendy nonsense is that supposed to be? They're going to ruin pan dulce, Luis!"

"Now who's catastrophizing?" Daddy joked gently. "It will be tough for a few months, but there's no way this place will stay open. Rose Hill locals know how to support each other. We'll just have to use the house savings to ride out the excitement of the opening."

Leo loved how Mamá and Daddy balanced each other, one calming if the other turned frantic, one seeing the bright side if the other was seeing the dark one.

"Are you sure about that?" Mamá asked. "Look at this: "Honeybees is the dream of Rose Hill's own native Belinda O'Rourke, who is so grateful to return to her hometown to begin her'—" Mamá let out a frustrated growl. "Belinda! That snake! I should have guessed she'd be behind this."

Leo winced. She didn't know anything about Belinda O'Rourke, but she was tired of discovering her family had all these enemies.

Daddy sighed deeply. "I thought she moved to . . . was it Chicago?"

"The day after graduation," Mamá fumed. "And then New York, and she's been in LA for years now. Don't look at me like that; the abuelas at church haven't stopped talking about her since high school. They're so *proud* just because she took off as soon as she could."

"And now she's coming back to town."

In the long silence, Leo waited for one of her parents to take the cheering-up role. Seconds ticked by, and her heart sank lower and lower, heavy with worry.

"I'd better go help the girls," Mamá said finally. "And I'll wash down the kitchen with manzanilla tonight. Maybe you can try . . ."

"Emailing the landlord," Daddy agreed quickly, "Sure. Maybe the business association as well. It can't hurt."

There was a worried hum and the smack of a besito, and Mamá appeared in the doorway, catching Leo off guard still pressed against the wall, with no chance to pretend she was just now passing by. She didn't want Mamá and Daddy to keep secrets, but she definitely didn't want to get caught stealing their secrets. Eyes squeezed shut, Leo waited for Mamá to see her, and her sharp voice to reverberate off the hallway walls.

Instead, Mamá stomped straight down the tiny hall into the kitchen. Leo opened her eyes in surprise. Good thing Mamá was so distracted! Before her luck could run out, Leo ducked into the bathroom on the other side of the hall. She leaned against the locked door, relief and frustration and worry making a marbled batter of her brain. Mamá had mentioned using chamomile, an herb that purged curses—did she think Abuelo Logroño had cursed them? What would happen if the bakery's customers all started eating Honeybees' bread and pastries instead? Leo thought about the old pizza restaurant, closed and forgotten, the building now ripped apart to make room for a new store. That couldn't happen to Amor y Azúcar—could it?

The colorful straw basket balanced on the toilet tank filled the bathroom with the scent of lavender and rosemary: calm and focus. Tía Paloma's herb blend, probably boosted with cinnamon power hidden with the molcajete. Generations of Leo's family members had come to this bathroom to worry, cry, or just rest during a long workday. Leo breathed deeply, the tightness around her heart easing. She and her family would come up with a plan to deal with all these problems. They had to.

Spirits buoyed, she unlocked the bathroom door and made her way back toward the kitchen.

And stepped straight into another disaster.

CHAPTER 9
ANOTHER DISASTER

Leo stood at the center of the kitchen, staring at the splatter of batter and dusting of dry ingredients that bloomed across the red tiles. A cooling rack had been upended, and broken puerquito bodies littered the floor. Isabel and Marisol stood with their backs to the counter, heads down.

". . . I've trusted you to act like young adults and help our family and our bakery be successful. . . ." Mamá's lecture flowed over the scene, sharp and disappointed and fast. "And that includes working out your differences. This is not how brujas act, and this is not how sisters act, and this is not how my daughters will act!"

Isabel clutched a metal mixing bowl in her batter-sticky hands, face red. "I'm sorry, Mamá," she said.

"It was an accident," Marisol added. "We were fighting, but I didn't mean to knock over all this stuff. I'm not even sure how it happened."

Mamá crossed her arms. "An accident? Isabel, is that true?"

Leo's oldest sister nodded. "Marisol wasn't anywhere near the counter," she said. "And I didn't touch anything, at least not at first. After the rack fell over, I tried to catch it, but . . . really, it was just a clumsy accident. We're sorry."

It would have taken a magic greater than Leo knew of to make her sisters lie to keep each other out of trouble. Mamá must have known the same, because she let out a sigh, rubbing her eyes with the heels of her hands. "Okay, it's all right, girls. Let's just get this all cleaned up." She glanced over her shoulder. "Oh, Leo, there you are. Would you grab the mop?"

Marisol swept and mopped the floor while Isabel and Mamá worked to restart the scheduled cake order, a chocolate birthday cake for the youngest Flores toddler, to be picked up at the end of the day. Leo sorted dirty dishes from the counters and the floor into the dishwasher before heading to the front to run the cash register.

"Thanks for the help, 'jita," Mamá said as she added conchas to the near-empty shelf and scanned the store for other items that needed to be restocked. "I know you wanted to meet up with your friends and your cousin. We're almost back on track here— just give it another half hour and you can go. What a wild day!"

"I know." Leo sighed. "I don't mind. I just want to help with . . . everything."

Marisol and Isabel would want to help too if they knew the worries Mamá and Daddy didn't want to share. She didn't mind working, but Leo felt sour frustration fill her stomach as she thought about all the secrets.

Mamá smiled. "Thank you, sweet girl. I'd better get started with more bolillos."

Leo was helping two regular customers with their after-lunch snacks when the rising voices of another kitchen argument filtered through the swinging blue doors.

Leo busied herself organizing receipts, hoping whatever had Marisol and Isabel upset would blow over, but when she heard her own name called out, she groaned and left the register to peek into the kitchen.

"What's wrong?"

Mamá and Marisol poked through the dishwasher shelves, muttering as it beeped in alarm at being opened halfway through its cycle.

"The bolillo mixing bowl is not supposed to go in the dishwasher, Leo." Isabel's voice was patient, but that only annoyed Leo more than anger would have. She wasn't a baby who needed to learn such basic lessons.

"I know that. I didn't put it in."

"You must have." Isabel said. "I left it in the sink before you cleared it out."

"Actually," Mamá said as she slammed the dishwasher closed, "it's not in here. Where else could you have left it, Isabel?"

Leo considered sticking out her tongue at her oldest sister. It wouldn't be the most mature or helpful thing to do, but snooty Isabel deserved it for thinking all mistakes had to be someone else's.

"But wait, I saw it in the sink too." Marisol frowned. "Nobody moved it?"

Everyone looked around the kitchen, the sudden silence dropping into Leo's stomach as every countertop and corner she scanned revealed no sign of the giant wooden bowl.

"Don't panic," Isabel squeaked, her voice panicked. "Let's look carefully. Maybe it got shuffled somewhere unexpected in the chaos."

They searched counters and cabinets, checked behind mixers and in every cranny of the walk-in fridge, but the bowl was nowhere to be found. Leo couldn't help thinking about the chaos a saltasombras could cause if he wanted to create a diversion in order to steal something. Could Abuelo Logroño be behind this? What would he want with their family heirloom?

Leo kept glancing at Mamá while she searched. Was this day full of terrible bad luck, or did all the bad news have a common source? And would Mamá tell Isabel and Marisol what was going on with the rent and the other bakery? Wasn't it only fair to share problems with everyone in the family, so that everyone could help think of solutions?

Marisol stopped searching first, throwing up her hands in the middle of the kitchen and then staying there until Isabel, Mamá, and finally Leo gravitated into her orbit, movement slowing until everyone stood in a frustrated clump.

"Well." Mamá looked around the kitchen with troubled eyes. "Maybe . . . maybe we close up early today and focus on prepping to have a calmer day tomorrow."

Leo opened her mouth to protest—closing down would mean losing a half day's profit!—but her voice didn't seem to be working, so all that came out was a squeak.

"I wouldn't mind," Isabel sighed. "Today needs a do-over." She shot an apologetic glance at Marisol, who scuffed her black boots against the floor and nodded.

"Leo, can you go get JP?" Mamá asked. "We'll probably be ready to drive home in an hour or so. Besides, Rita would hate to hear that we sent him gallivanting around town alone all day."

"He's not gallivanting alone," Leo said. "He's with Caroline and Brent at the library, playing Catan." But she pulled off her hat and untied her apron. She wished she could brush away her worries as easily as she shook flour off her shorts.

"Don't worry." Isabel patted down Leo's disheveled hat hair. "I'm sure the bowl will turn up. We're all just worn out and cranky right now."

"Why don't you big girls clean up and start the dough for tomorrow morning?" Mamá asked. "I'm going to update your father and check on something." She smiled weakly, pulled a mechanical pencil out of thin air, and snagged a bag of dried chamomile on her way past the back cabinets.

Mamá was clearly suspicious that the disappearing bowl might be the result of bad magic. Why didn't she say something?

Leo didn't want to leave the bakery, but she couldn't think of anything more useful to do, so eventually she wandered out the front door, helping herself to the last dried-out puerquito on the shelf. She'd had no time to add piñata frosting, but the less-sugary treat was better for eating and walking anyway, since it didn't make her mouth quite so sticky and thirsty.

The walk to the library should have been a nice one. The April afternoon was pleasantly warm and the sky stretched wide and blue behind dollops of white whipped-cream clouds. But instead of warming up Leo's mood, the beautiful day burned the thin worried edges of her heart. The shops lining Main Street suddenly felt more threatening than familiar, each business's bright spring window display competing to draw customers away from Amor y Azúcar. Colorful awnings striped the sidewalk in shadow, and Leo moved through the patches of light and dark with the creeping feeling that someone was following close behind her or watching her from around every corner. She shivered, suddenly cold in spite of the sun.

By the time she reached the library, she was almost running and wanted nothing more than to escape into a board game with her cousin and her friends.

Leo slipped through the clear glass doors of Rose Hill Library silently, not even getting a glance from the librarians sitting at the circulation desk. She inhaled the dusty old-book air with a smile. Daddy always brought Leo and her sisters here as soon as school let out for the year, challenging them to check out enough books that the stack would reach above Daddy's head when he tried to carry it by himself. During the school year most of Leo's books came from the school library or Caroline's bookshelf—being in the public library always felt like summer.

The sound of hushed giggling led Leo to a table where Caroline, Brent, and JP sat by a stack of board games. Settlers of Catan was spread on the table, the hexagonal board forming a colorful island for players to build roads and houses on.

"I'm just saying, if we're the settlers, then what happened to the indigenous people of Catan?" JP asked. "Maybe the so-called robber is actually trying to decolonize the land."

"Good point." Brent nodded sadly. "It's like when Ms. Wood told us the truth about Columbus Day."

"My mom's been telling me about that stuff since I was in pre-K," JP said. "She's a professor."

Leo came up to the table, but no one even looked her way.

"My prima in Costa Rica is like that," Caroline said. "She gets really excited talking about Juan Santamaría and how the Central American alliance kept the US invaders away."

"Is that the same cousin who's learning candle m—" Leo caught herself before saying magic in front of JP. "Traditions with you?"

"Invaders from the US?" Brent asked, ignoring Leo and leaning right in front of her. "When did the US invade anyone? Why didn't we learn this in history?"

"Um, guys?" Leo asked, annoyed at her friends. They had spent all day with JP; any starstruck feelings they had about an out-of-towner should have worn off by now. And besides, ignoring someone was just rude.

"It's your turn," Caroline told Brent, and the three turned back to the board to collect their resources as Brent rolled the dice. Not one of them acknowledged the fourth person at the table.

This wasn't rudeness. This was something else.

She waved her hand in front of Brent's face, then

leaned across the table to do the same to Caroline. No reaction.

"Are you ignoring me on purpose?" Leo asked hopefully. Once, when she was only five or six years old, Leo had played along with a prank Alma and Belén had cooked up to ignore JP, because he had accidentally spilled juice on their new coloring book. Even when JP stood right in front of them, face red and eyes watering, Leo had stared straight ahead until Mamá caught on and lectured her and the twins about how they should treat others. Leo still felt guilty remembering it.

There was a chance that JP had dragged Caroline and Brent into an elaborate plot to get revenge for that childhood cruelty. But it seemed like a very small chance.

JP rolled a seven and reached over the board so that his hand nearly bumped Leo's elbow. She moved away by instinct but then thought better of it. When JP picked up the gray robber figurine, Leo quickly snatched it out of his hand and held it tight in her fist.

"Uy!" JP snatched his hand back and waved it in the air. "I think something just bit me!"

"A bug?" Brent asked. "I didn't see anything."

"Let me look?" Caroline leaned over to inspect JP's hand.

"It doesn't hurt, but it scared me," he said. "I dropped the robber; I'm afraid I lost it."

"I'll find it!" Brent dropped to the floor to search the carpet while Caroline cooed sympathetically over JP's hand. Leo stood in the middle of it all, the cold she had felt just before walking into the library suddenly digging into her gut. The robber dropped from her hand.

"Found it!" Brent crawled up from under the table and triumphantly waved the robber. "I'm a Hufflepuff," he said, by explanation.

As the conversation turned to house identity and eventually back to Catan, Leo felt tears prick the back of her throat.

She was *invisible*.

Then the watery feeling froze into a hard lump of understanding. She knew exactly who she needed. The same person who was behind all of today's horribleness, the only person she knew with the power to turn invisible.

It was time to talk to him.

CHAPTER 10
ABUELO'S PLAN

The library had plenty of quiet, tucked-away corners for studying, so Leo found one close to the shelf of books for young readers. The familiar covers and spines gave her courage as she checked that the coast was clear, took a deep breath, and called out, "Abuelo?"

She was afraid heads would turn and someone would come running to shush her, but the librarians couldn't hear her any more than her friends could. ·She counted to three before trying again. "Abuelo Logroño? Where are you? I'm ready to talk."

She waited, eyes bouncing around the corners of

the room as she chewed on her bottom lip. Hadn't her abuelo said to call if she wanted to ask him questions? Was there a magic calling spell she was supposed to know? Or had he decided that she wasn't worth talking to now that she had told Mamá about his visit? Leo clenched her fists. She wouldn't want to talk to him either, if there was anyone else she knew who could help her with this problem.

There was a crash from the front of the library. Leo startled, but the library patrons she could see didn't lift their heads out of their books at the sound, or at the slap of footsteps running through the aisles. Leo craned her neck to see the strange sight of Abuelo Logroño running through the library, his arms flailing and his black robe flapping wildly around him, revealing a pair of old worn-out green flip-flops on his gnarled feet. Leo would have laughed, except that he was running full tilt at her.

Before she could jump out of the way of her surprisingly speedy grandfather, he skidded to an ungainly stop just a few feet in front of her. He panted a bit, arranged the folds of his robe to hide his shoes, then smoothed his ruffled gray hair and cleared his throat.

"What are you *doing*?" Leo asked.

"Uy!" Abuelo Logroño hopped in place and looked

over his shoulder before meeting Leo's gaze with a suspicious squint. "You can see me?" he asked.

"You can see *me*?" Leo responded, crossing her arms.

"Well, of course I . . . oh." Abuelo Logroño suddenly shuffled closer to peer at Leo's face. "Are you . . . ?"

"Invisible!" Leo threw up her hands. "And I don't know how it happened, or what to do about it, but you said you know all about it, so help me fix it!"

". . . jamás en la vida creí que vería . . ." Abuelo broke into a smile so huge that Leo took a step back in surprise. "You've made your first jump already! With barely a nudge! This kind of power in my family—I've been waiting my whole life for this! And to find it in you of all people, a little girl!"

Leo found herself enveloped by the huge puffy sleeves of Abuelo's robe, a hug that felt cold and smelled like old coins. She shook herself free, glaring at Abuelo's grin.

"Don't you see?" he continued. "You must study with me. You're born for it, like a fish for water!"

Leo pressed her lips together. "Is this my birth-order power? I turn invisible? I can't even make my friends see me when I want to—this feels more like a curse!"

Abuelo Logroño's smile shrank. "Your power as a saltasombras is the legacy of your Logroño family. It is our birthright and destiny. It is not a curse. And your abilities will go beyond the silly parlor tricks of your mother's lineage—if you let me train you."

If Abuelo Logroño wasn't going to stop being rude, then Leo could be rude right back. "You're not going to train me in anything. You're going to tell me how to turn this invisibility off, and then you're going to leave me alone."

"I don't see why I would want to do that," Abuelo Logroño said. "It makes no difference to me if you stay invisible for a few hours or a few years."

Leo glared. "Then I'll figure it out myself."

"Saltasombras powers are notoriously difficult to control. Once you reappear, you might never be able to use your powers again without my help."

Leo stomped her foot. "I know all about you, and I know that my mamá banished you with her magic, and if you don't leave us alone, then we'll cook up something even worse for you."

Abuelo Logroño didn't look happy anymore. He picked lint off the edge of his sleeve and breathed loudly through his nose. "You're referring to those little warding spells on your house and your bakery, I assume? Terrifying. I'm shaking in my boots."

"Flip-flops," Leo corrected. Abuelo frowned and shifted his weight as he pulled his toes back under his robe.

"The fact of the matter," he continued, "is that even if your family had the guts to hex me, which I very much doubt they do, they have bigger problems to deal with now. Like running their business properly, while they can."

Leo was often frustrated, and she didn't always hold her temper when she was upset. She got mad at her sisters, annoyed at her parents, and sick of Señor Gato lying on her books. She had once been so irritated by Brent's rudeness that she had cast a spell on him, with disastrous results. But she wasn't used to feeling anger unsweetened by love. She wasn't used to the way fear bled in like spice magic, turning rage strong and bitter. It felt almost like magic singing through her veins—but a magic she didn't like.

"Why don't you leave us alone?" Leo demanded.

"Oh dear, have I struck a nerve?" Abuelo Logroño smirked while Leo blinked to keep her wet eyes from spilling over. "That's the trouble with your antepasada and her clever loophole. It's a rather shaky foundation to build your magic on."

"What are you talking about?" Leo blinked a few times but made sure not to drop her death glare. "My five-times-great-grandma bound her magic and passed it down to her family. She started the recipe book, the initiation, and the bakery."

"Yes, a bunch of piecemeal traditions to try to make up for the fact that she had no family name to pass down," Abuelo said. "Now your magic depends on those bulky inventions, housed inside that *bakery* of yours." He spat out the word like it tasted bad. "And your mamá thinks she can lock you away from your real birthright. But you've proven that isn't true."

A librarian came down the aisle with a cart of books. When she got close to Abuelo Logroño, she stopped, shivered, and then walked around him without seeming to realize she was doing it. Leo watched her go, wishing she could avoid her abuelo so easily. But he was the only person who could see her, and she still had no idea how to fix that.

"Magic is a difficult force to grasp, you know," Abuelo Logroño said as he watched the librarian hurry to a different aisle. "Existing throughout the world just outside of human reach, but not so far away that we can't sense it."

"Part of everything," Leo whispered, thinking of Abuela's spirit. It gave her courage to remember that Abuela existed everywhere, even right here and now, when Leo felt so confused and alone.

"Directionless and diffuse," Abuelo Logroño scoffed. "Weak. Through studying, brujos of old found ways to access and channel magic, standardize it somewhat, and create clear rules and guidelines. Before those discoveries, magic would crop up wherever humans happened to stumble upon it, with no logic or will behind it."

"Everyone has different aptitudes," Leo said. Abuela had once told her that magic touched people's lives in different ways. "What's wrong with that?"

"Not much, if your biggest worry is a collapsed cake." Abuelo Logroño smirked. "But I told you, we are weapons to protect humanity, and we must be at our sharpest."

"Why?" Leo asked. "Do you really go around fighting people all the time?"

"Not people," Abuelo Logroño snapped, "Creatures that haunt this land and try to pass as human beings. They're dangerous; they can't be trusted to live among us. We find them, expose them. We're not heartless; whenever possible we try to send these dangerous creatures to other realms or to places where humans don't live. It's the way we have kept humanity safe for hundreds of years. It's the way it has to be done."

"Mamá says they're not hurting anyone," Leo said.

"Your mother is naive!" Abuelo Logroño shouted.

He took a few deep breaths, flattening his hair and shaking out his robes. "As I was saying, brujos of old continued to experiment, and they found a way to bind their magic to a certain course. It could be passed down a family line through a shared name."

That sounded like her family's magic, passed down from mothers to daughters, but Leo refused to ask any more questions. Abuelo Logroño kept talking anyway.

"Names have always carried power, of course, and brujos of old took steps to ensure that the names they used would carry specific magical abilities to future generations. Names are stable, connecting new brujos to their ancestors through law and tradition. With magic tied to these lasting institutions, finally progress could be made. Brujo families consolidated power and knowledge, each generation training its offspring. Your ancestor couldn't pass on her name, so she decided she knew better than every brujo before her."

Leo didn't understand why he sounded so angry about that. Her antepasada had done something original, and now Leo's family could bring love and magic to the town. Wasn't that more important than some old tradition?

"Our Logroño powers can be traced back through the fifteenth century, before our ancestors left Spain to bring magical balance to this continent."

Leo frowned. She had never thought about her family coming from Spain, even though they spoke Spanish. Abuelo Logroño seemed proud of the heritage, but Aunt Rita and Ms. Wood talked about how much harm Christopher Columbus and others like him had done when they first came to this hemisphere. What did that mean about her ancestors?

"I could teach you about your noble pedigree," Abuelo Logroño said. "Logroño is your primary name, of course, coming from your father's father's father and so forth. But you carry other strains of magic in your apellidos."

"I don't need to know all my last names to know my power," Leo said. Mamá didn't have the same last name as Tía Paloma, and neither of them had the same name as their grandmother.

"These legacies carry centuries of power." Abuelo frowned. "They have given us some of the strongest brujería the world has ever seen. You mother's power, her ancestor's experiment, is a trivial footnote, one that may soon come to an end."

"Our magic isn't going anywhere," Leo said.

"Maybe not. But in the absence of a name to

carry power, your antepasada had to bind her magic to something. And physical things, books, bowls, bakeries—well, magic that's tied to those sorts of objects can only last while the object does." Abuelo shrugged dramatically. "Oh, but I'm sure you're right. Your mother's magic will last forever. Just like her business."

Cold fear tickled the back of Leo's neck. Abuelo Logroño knew that the business was in danger. He must be the one behind the money troubles, just like Mamá suspected. And now Leo knew why he was doing it: an attack on the bakery was an attack on the family magic.

"By all means, warn all your sisters and your mother about me," he said. "Put up a ward ten times more powerful. I think you'll find my accomplices unimpressed."

Accomplices? Caroline's dad sometimes called Leo "my daughter's favorite accomplice," so Leo knew it meant a partner in crime. What accomplices did Abuelo Logroño have? She felt like she was moving in slow motion while Abuelo Logroño ran circles around her with his knowledge and plotting.

"You'd better think about what you want, young Logroño, or soon enough you might find your powers disappearing. And then you'll come to me begging for training. So think hard before you make an enemy out of your last hope. . . ."

He took a shuffling step to the side, the air around him rippling, but instead of disappearing into thin air, he stepped back into sight, causing the librarian, who had just reappeared with her cart, to shriek and drop a stack of books. Abuelo cursed, stepped back into the shadows of invisibility, gave Leo one last parting glare, and then stalked unglamorously down the aisle, flip-flops smacking the carpet as he went.

Even though she was terrified and angry and tearful—or maybe because of all that—Leo couldn't help but snort at the awkward figure he made in his robe, like a bird whose body didn't quite know how to move on the ground. The snort popped out of her mouth like the plug of an inflatable pool toy, and a stream of laughter followed, flowing from the pit of worry in her stomach and warming her as it left. It felt good to laugh in spite of the scary things. Leo felt like she couldn't stop.

The librarian who had disappeared after her scare was now scolding someone nearby, her voice floating through the aisles of bookshelves. "Young lady," the stern voice kept saying. It made Leo laugh even harder.

"Young lady!" The librarian rounded a corner and stood face-to-face with Leo, just where Abuelo Logroño had been moments before. Surprise quieted Leo's laugh. "What exactly is so funny?" The librarian, who Leo recognized from her visits to the bakery, frowned straight at Leo, the bright pins on her jean jacket and red stripes in her black hair making her angry face extra intimidating. She looked like the person Marisol would want to grow up to be, complete with Marisol's grumpy annoyance with Leo.

"You can hear me?" Leo asked.

"The whole library can hear you," the librarian chided. "Please keep it down. If I catch you at it again, I'll have to let your parents know."

Leo probably should have pretended to be worried about the threat, but all she could do was grin. The librarian could see her! "Yes, ma'am," Leo whispered. Then she took off toward the board-game table.

"No running," the librarian sighed behind her, but Leo was in too much of a hurry to listen.

CHAPTER 11
REVELATION

"Leo, there you are!" JP was the first to spot her. "What took you so long?"

"Sorry," she said. "It got really busy at the bakery. I'm actually coming to get you because we're going to head home soon."

"You didn't miss too much," Brent informed her. "Except that the Queen of Catan finally lost a game."

"I was trying to be nice," Caroline grumbled. "It was JP's first time playing, so I was being generous with swapping materials and giving him advice, and then he totally betrayed me!"

"It's not betrayal to keep your victory points

hidden until the end," Brent said. "That's *your* usual strategy."

"I really like this!" JP said. "It's all mind games, and you have to think strategically. If you play a certain way one round, you have to switch it up the next, or you're going to get beat."

Leo looked at the game board. Whatever was happening with Abuelo Logroño was a type of mind game, which meant she had to start thinking strategically. She had to figure out Abuelo's plan—and how to stop it—without letting him know she was on to him. She knew he wasn't working alone now, thanks to his mention of accomplices, so maybe she could start her investigation there.

"Leo?" Caroline asked. "Is everything okay?"

"Her brain is still at the bakery," Brent said. "As usual."

She gave Caroline a look. If she planned to do any kind of strategic planning to outsmart her abuelo, she needed to consult the Queen of Catan.

Caroline, always an excellent accomplice, picked up on her hint. "If we're heading out, Leo, do you want to help me return this to the circulation desk?"

"Are you sure we don't have time for one more game?" JP asked. "Or are you afraid of how badly we'd beat you with a Logroño cousin alliance?"

The way he smirked and used their family name sounded too much like Abuelo Logroño, and Leo found herself snapping, "Who says I'd be teaming up with you?"

While Brent *ooh*ed into his fist, Leo grabbed the packed-up game box from Caroline's hands and flounced away, leaving the boys to a playful shoving match.

"What's up?" Caroline asked when they were out of earshot.

"A lot." Leo sighed. "My grandpa is even worse than we thought, and he has a plan to destroy the bakery and our whole line of family magic. And I think he stole our bolillo mixing bowl!"

Caroline's eyebrows arched. "Can he do that?"

"Destroy our magic? I don't know. But my parents are really worried about competition from this new bakery, and I think he might be behind that too. And maybe also something with our new landlord?" There were so many problems and possibilities that she needed to investigate. "And that's not even the biggest thing I needed to tell you!"

She was about to explain to her best friend how she had discovered her power of invisibility, and what it might mean, when JP's voice came from somewhere close behind them.

"Did they get lost? Do you think Leo's avoiding me?"

"I'm sure she isn't," Brent answered. "How could anyone want to—I mean, why would she avoid you?"

"Uh-oh, incoming." Caroline pulled Leo toward the front desk. "Tell me quickly?"

Leo's tongue tangled around the news. She didn't want to reveal her new power here, in line at the library circulation desk. She wanted to have time to tell the story, and she wanted Caroline to have time to listen. "Can we talk tomorrow?" she asked. "Come by the bakery early so we can plan?"

"Sure," Caroline said. "I love plans. Um . . . will JP be there?"

Leo sighed. "You aren't going to ask me to make another love potion, are you?"

Caroline flushed. "I never *asked* you to do the first . . . I'm not even . . . Brent is the one who won't shut up about how cool JP is, and his muscles!"

Leo scrunched her face and stuck out her tongue. "He doesn't have *muscles*; he's my cousin."

"Well, Brent is way more obvious," Caroline muttered, twirling her butterfly ring.

"I'm way more what?"

Brent and JP caught up just in time to see Caroline's face turn an even darker shade of red.

"More obnoxious," Leo said.

"Ouch. Leo's cranky today," JP teased back, and the four of them joked their way to the circulation desk and then out of the library.

At the bike rack outside, Caroline and Brent buckled their helmets and gripped their handlebars.

"See you tomorrow?" Leo asked Caroline.

Brent broke out into an immediate grin. "Are we doing this again tomorrow? Awesome. It gets boring being off school for the whole week. We should keep hanging out."

"Um, sure," Leo said. Maybe Brent coming along would be good, if he could distract JP.

Caroline and Brent waved and pedaled away toward their neighborhood, leaving Leo and JP to walk the few blocks back to the bakery.

"You know," JP said as they went, "it's okay if you were trying to get rid of me today. I know you and Marisol were busy this morning and I wasn't helping very much. It's cool to see how the bakery works and everything, but I checked out a couple of comics on Caroline's library card, so I can definitely make myself more scarce from now on. I'm not trying to annoy you."

Now Leo felt guilty. "No, I'm sorry we were so busy," she said. "That's not usually how things are. We're sort of stressed right now."

"The pest problem?" JP asked. "And the new bakery?"

Leo nodded. They approached Amor y Azúcar, and she could see that the front-door sign had been flipped to *CLOSED*. Through the window, the empty shelves gaped at them, like a bad omen.

JP zipped and unzipped the main pocket of his fanny pack. "Yeah. Before my mom got tenure at her college, there were a few times when she didn't know what was going to happen with her department. We had to move when she lost her job in Houston. It's not fun."

Leo nodded. "I'm sorry I said I wouldn't be part of your Catan alliance. I was mad at . . . other things, not at you."

JP smiled. "Thanks. I was afraid for a second that maybe you didn't really want me to stay here for the whole week."

"I was afraid you didn't want to stay here with Alma and Belén gone," Leo admitted. "But Brent *was* right. It gets totally boring around here on breaks."

"You should come stay in Austin sometime," JP said. "Even if none of our bakeries can compete."

Leo grinned, then sighed. Thinking of competing bakeries made her think of Honeybees, which made a heavy lump reappear in her stomach. She had to find a way to stop Abuelo, but she didn't know where to start, and she didn't want to keep making JP feel bad by not spending time with him. The more she thought about all the secrets, the colder and heavier she felt, like she was being swallowed by a cloud of foggy bad feeling.

"Whoa," JP said.

"What?" Leo pulled her gaze up from the sidewalk.

"You didn't . . . There was something weird with the light. It looked all wavy, like you were . . . Never mind." He shook his head. "I must have imagined it."

Leo shrugged, knocking on the locked bakery door.

"Welcome back," Daddy said as he opened it. "Hope you had a good time at the library. Leo, your mamá wanted to talk to you."

"Did she find the bowl?" Leo asked hopefully.

Daddy shook his head. "Not yet, but you know what they say: the dough must go on!" Daddy's goofy grin and JP's loud chuckle helped pop the bubble of worry around Leo's head.

"Mamá?" she said, running into the kitchen.

"Back here."

Leo followed the voice to the office, where Mamá

sat in front of two lit candles and two mugs of tea. Leo sniffed the air. Chamomile.

"Sit down," Mamá said. "I didn't really get to talk to you about . . . everything. How are you handling it all?"

Leo breathed the calming smell of candle smoke and steam and smiled. Finally she and Mamá could share their secrets and work on tackling the problem together. "Well, I talked to Abuelo Logroño again, and I learned a lot—"

"You what?" Mamá spilled tea on her apron and yelped. "Why did you talk to him? Leo, how did he find you? The ward we set up should keep him from being able to locate you. If it's not working, we need to know."

"No, Mamá—I called him," Leo said. "And I think the ward did work, because it took him a lot longer to answer this time."

"You called him?" If Mamá hadn't set down her tea she might have spilled it again. "'Jita, what were you thinking? He's dangerous!"

"I know, Mamá!" Leo said, exasperated. She closed her eyes, took a deep breath, and squared her shoulders. "Listen. I got information from him. He wants me to train with him really badly, and I think he's messing with the bakery as a way to pressure me into it. And he's not working alone. But I think we can fight back."

"Leo." Mamá rubbed her hands over her face. "I don't want you to have anything to do with Álvaro, and I certainly don't want you fighting him. Please, leave this to me. You are absolutely not to contact him again."

"I wasn't going to! I'm strategizing."

"Stop strategizing," Mamá ordered. "None of this is your concern. We put wards up against your grandfather, and as long as no one goes calling him again, they will hold. That's the end of it."

"But Mamá—"

"But nothing. Drink your manzanilla."

"To cleanse me from bad magic, right?" Leo snapped. "You're worried too, I know you are. And what about Honeybees? A bakery just happens to be opening that just happens to have our same menu?"

Mamá looked up sharply. "Who told you that?"

Leo swallowed. She had been about to bring up the rent as well, but remembered that she wasn't supposed to have overheard Mamá and Daddy before. "Nobody, I . . . we looked it up on Caroline's phone. Mamá, what if that's part of Abuelo's plan? Or what if there are other threats to the business? Shouldn't we be able to use magic to stop all of that?"

"Leonora Elena!" Her mother's voice was sharp. "If that's what you think magic is for, then you haven't learned the most important thing I've been trying to teach you. Our magic is love. We are not going to attack another business out of fear."

Leo hung her head. It wasn't as if Mamá had ever exactly told Leo that she shouldn't use magic to hurt others, but that was because she'd never had to. Leo knew that the way she knew she shouldn't punch other people when she got angry. But . . . "What if they're using magic against us?"

"I've known Belinda O'Rourke since I was younger than you are now," Mamá said. "Her grandmother babysat me. We ran against each other for class president, were always competing for class rank. . . . She's not my favorite person in the world, but she's not evil, she's certainly not a spell caster, and I can't see any possible way she could be working with your abuelo."

"But shouldn't we at least investigate? What if—"

"Drop it, Leo. You are not attacking Honeybees with magic. You are not attacking anyone with magic. You are not worrying about any of this, because the only thing you need to know is that I'm handling it." She turned back to her tea, let out a long sigh, then pulled an extra sugar packet out of the air to add to the mug. Leo lifted her tea and burned her tongue, frustrated tears threatening to spill. She knew Mamá and Daddy were worried. She knew they suspected that Abuelo Logroño was plotting from the shadows. Why wouldn't they tell her? More secrets, more lies.

Well, if Mamá wasn't going to do anything, then Leo would. She just didn't know what.

"Are you kids getting hungry?" Daddy asked when she stomped back into the front of the store. "I was going to head home and start dinner while Elena finishes here."

"Definitely!" JP said.

There was a huge steaming pot that smelled like chamomile in the kitchen. Mamá was probably going to scrub the whole bakery. But Leo wasn't supposed to know or care anything about that. "Fine," she said. She followed her cousin into Daddy's truck.

"I hope you're ready to learn the legendary Logroño family quesadilla recipe," Daddy said to JP as the truck rattled away from downtown Rose Hill. "There aren't many people I would trust with my most valuable cooking secrets."

Leo rolled her eyes from the back seat. "It's not very secret," she said. "It's just cheese. Plus all the, you know, salsa and crema and pico de gallo and everything you put on at the end."

"Spoken like someone who doesn't know the legendary Logroño family recipe," Daddy said. "Passed down for . . . well, not passed down for any generations, really."

Leo paused thinking about that. "Grandma Logroño didn't teach you to make quesadillas?"

"Oh, she might have." Daddy shrugged. "Okay, so passed down for one generation maybe."

"But"—Leo felt annoyance itching the back of her throat—"didn't she learn to make quesadillas from somewhere? Maybe from her mom?"

"If so, I never heard anything about it. Who's to say?"

"It wouldn't be a Logroño family recipe, though," JP pointed out.

"Good point." Daddy nodded. "The legendary Logroño-Hernandez-Mayo . . . hmm, this is getting a little too complicated. Better forget the whole thing."

A sense of unfairness pinched Leo's chest. Why did names work this way in the first place, making it easy to name a whole family of men but impossible to name things passed down by women? She wondered if this was the feeling that made her five-times-great-grandmother start her own family line of magical brujas.

A red light stopped the truck in the shadow of a tall oleander bush, the white flowers blooming against the reflection of Leo's fuming face in the window. As her thoughts kept twisting into gloomy knots, the image on the window flickered and shimmered. But just as quickly, the flicker was gone, and it was only her reflected face again among the oleander blossoms.

She thought about the danger the bakery was in, the danger of Abuelo Logroño's plot. Her stomach grew heavy and goose bumps pricked her arms as she focused on her sadness. And—there!—her reflection flickered away once more in a shimmer of shadow, leaving a split second of plain white flowers.

Leo laughed in surprise, and her face reappeared. She stared at her wide eyes, heart pounding. Sadness, frustration, heavy feelings that weighed her down . . . they seemed tied to her powers. Could it really be that easy?

"What do you think of your cousin's idea, Leonora?" Daddy looked in the rearview mirror with a grimace. "I'm not sure how it would taste to cook whole tomato slices into the quesadilla. It sounds more like a grilled cheese."

"Trust me," JP said, "it's good. I can show you."

"I guess there's no harm in trying something new," Daddy said. "Maybe your way will become a legendary Logroño family recipe, passed down for generations."

Leo's tiny sigh caused another ripple on the window. She was still scared, but also, just maybe, the tiniest bit excited. She had a clue how to control her birth-order power, and she hadn't needed Abuelo Logroño's help to figure it out. That was something no one had expected. It was like a hidden card in Catan, a power she could use to her advantage, a shadowy secret Mamá didn't even know about.

She just needed to get better at it. Abuelo Logroño and anyone he was working with wouldn't know what hit them.

CHAPTER 12
PRACTICE AND PLOTS

Mamá told Leo she didn't need to help open the bakery early with her and Isabel and Marisol the next morning, but Leo didn't sleep in. As soon as the car pulled out of the driveway, Leo was up and practicing in front of the mirror.

For the first fifteen minutes she was so nervous that she couldn't manage to make so much as a pinkie go blurry. But after a half hour, she started to be able to tap that heavy, sad, frightened feeling in the pit of her stomach, the one that made the air around her grow cold and shimmery. And by the time Daddy knocked to see if she wanted breakfast,

Leo could—with enough concentration—make her reflection shimmer and blink out of sight for about two seconds at a time.

It wasn't exactly power beyond her wildest dreams, but it was a start.

With the excuse of wanting to check the library hours, Leo borrowed JP's phone during breakfast and googled Honeybees Café as a starting place for her investigation. The website was everything Leo had already overheard, plus an irritating pale green and neon yellow color scheme. More interesting was an article on the *Rose Hill Chronicle*'s site: an interview with Belinda O'Rourke, the West Coast entrepreneur returning home to Texas at last.

Leo stared at the pale and brightly made-up face of the Honeybees owner. Was it just Leo's imagination, or did the wide smile and light brown curls feel like they hid something sinister? Leo scrolled down to the middle of the interview.

Rose Hill Chronicle: Why did you want to open up Honeybees here in Rose Hill?

Belinda O'Rourke: I came up with the idea for this café years ago, but it seemed like it would be impossible to get off the ground, so I never pursued it. And in the meantime, I was busy raising my daughter, trying to give her the life I always thought I wanted. But eventually I missed my roots, and I wanted Becky to have a connection to my home-town. It wasn't until after I decided to move back that I started thinking about all the possibilities the move would open up for me, and that's when I remembered my old dream of opening a café.

Belinda O'Rourke cared about family tradi-tions—did that mean she could ally with someone like Abuelo Logroño? But, Leo thought, Mamá would probably agree about the importance of honoring your roots. In fact, it sounded like Mrs. O'Rourke wasn't as much of a big-city snob as Mamá thought. Or was all the love for Rose Hill just a lie she was telling for the interview?

Rose Hill Chronicle: There's a food component to your café as well. Can you tell the town what they can expect from that side of the business?

Belinda O'Rourke: I think they can expect to see familiar favorites with an updated twist. I didn't want to serve the same things your grandmother would eat—I want to bring all my life experiences together to create a real fusion of flavors and culi-nary traditions from the places I've seen in my travels. We're mixing up something very special for y'all here.

"Um, is everything okay?" JP interrupted Leo's researching, startling her.

"What? Yes, why?"

"I don't know, you looked really annoyed," JP said, holding out his hand for his phone.

Leo quickly closed the interview. "Oh, yeah, no. I just . . . couldn't find the opening time. But Caroline will probably know it." She passed the phone back to her cousin, forcing a smile.

Never mind what she'd thought a moment ago. Mamá was right about Belinda O'Rourke. She was nothing but a snob who cared about Rose Hill only enough to want to change it to be more like somewhere else. She could definitely be Abuelo Logroño's accomplice. They both even liked to insult other people's grandmas!

Riding to the bakery with Daddy, Leo kept chewing on the words from the interview. Something else was bothering her about the cheery way Mrs. O'Rourke ended her answer. But it wasn't until she stepped inside the bakery and smelled the fresh bolillos coming out of the oven that it occurred to her.

We're mixing up *something very special.*

Of course. Mrs. O'Rourke had every reason to steal Amor y Azúcar's mixing bowl. Not only would it help Abuelo's plot to hurt the bakery, but it would also give a boost of stolen magic to Honeybees' baking.

"Still no luck with the bowl," Isabel told Daddy in a hushed voice, "But even so, I think these bolillos are looking okay."

Leo eyed the big plastic bin of bolillos. They did look like they usually did, but there was something a little less inviting about the colors and shapes of this batch—like Leo had baked them instead of Mamá. She leaned over and sniffed. Not bad, but not quite perfect.

She would just have to get the mixing bowl back as soon as possible. And now she knew where to look.

In an effort to be more welcoming to JP, Leo had decided to give him a guided tour of the kitchen. He thought the walk-in fridge was super cool, and was fascinated watching Mamá making conchas.

"So you make a whole other dough to put on top of the first dough? Does that mean a concha is secretly a sandwich?"

Leo decided not to tell him about ojos de buey.

Marisol generously offered to let JP help with her

job of taking cooled pastries out to the shelves, and Isabel showed him how she piped frosting onto the border of a tres leches cake. Mamá even let him stir one of her batters, just like Leo used to do when she was tiny.

"How's it going?" Daddy asked JP when he emerged from the office to open the store for the morning. "The girls aren't overwhelming you with all the kitchen talk, are they?"

"Daddy." Marisol rolled her eyes. "You're not going to pretend to be all macho just because JP is here, are you?"

"Yeah, that was sort of sexist," Isabel said.

"I like cooking," JP said. "And I want to learn more about baking; it seems really cool, even though it's hard. And you didn't think I was overwhelmed by kitchen talk when we made quesadillas."

Daddy shook his head fast back and forth like Señor Gato when he got water on his whiskers. "You're right! Sorry, everyone. I thought Rita and Elena had trained all the gender stereotyping out of me, but I guess there's always more to chip away at."

"Keep up your guard, friend of dragons," JP said, making Daddy laugh. He patted Leo's baseball cap, and just like that, a feeling of calm replaced the gnawing hurt that had been lodged in Leo's chest. It almost felt like Isabel's power of influence changing Leo's emotions, but the only magic her sisters had used was the magic of speaking up when something didn't sound right to them. It was a power Leo was eager to learn.

A few minutes later, Isabel was supervising Daddy and JP's cookie-cutter contest, making sure that in their race to finish the most puerquitos they didn't roll the dough unevenly or cut off any tiny pig legs. Leo jumped up from her post at the register when Caroline and Brent burst into the bakery, bringing the warmth of the spring morning in with them.

"How's business?" Caroline asked when Daddy came out to say hello. "Did Leo give you my candle?"

Daddy tapped the burning green candle in the tall glass on the counter. "Not much to report since yesterday, but we're confident that everything will go in our favor."

"Oh, good," Brent said. "Does that mean my breakfast can still be on the house?"

Once they each had a concha in hand, Leo and JP led their friends out to sit on the curb so nobody would spy on them and they wouldn't bother the customers. "What's the plan for today?" JP asked.

"Well . . ." Caroline looked at Leo, who looked back

at Caroline blankly. How were they going to ditch the boys long enough for Leo to explain her new power and plan a top-secret investigation mission?

"We could go to Caroline's house," Brent said. "It's not too far, and she has a trampoline. Plus I'm next door so we can play Mario Kart at my house."

"Sounds good." JP smiled. "You're coming this time, right, Leo?"

"Yes . . . but why don't you and Brent go ahead of us? I have to show Caroline . . . something. We'll catch up! Soon!"

Both Brent and JP fixed their eyes on her with matching suspicious expressions.

"What do you want to show Caroline but not us?" Brent asked.

"Brent." Caroline put her hand on his elbow. "It's not a big deal. It's just a . . . special thing that Leo only wants to talk to me about."

Brent raised an eyebrow in confusion for a moment, then seemed to realize something. "Okay!" he squeaked in a terrible attempt to sound casual. "Catch y'all later!"

"Wait—is that all?" JP said. He unzipped a side pocket of his fanny pack and pulled out a square of wrinkly pink plastic wrapping. "I can help with that."

"JP," Leo groaned. "I do not need a pad."

Her cousin shrugged and returned the menstrual pad to his pouch. "My friends from school sometimes need them, so I started carrying one, for emergencies. What else are you being so secretive about then?"

"Not menstruation." Caroline's face was red again, but she shot Leo a nod before she continued. "It's actually a . . . present. That we were planning for a friend. That we have to do this week before he, uh, I mean *they*, leave."

Leo could see what Caroline was trying to do, and played along. "Shh!" She giggled, elbowing Caroline. "You'll ruin it!"

"Okay, um, sure," Brent said. He wasn't quite as good at catching on to Caroline's schemes, but he knew enough to support them. "JP, let's . . . go play video games. They're being weird anyway."

JP looked at them all awkwardly, then turned to follow Brent.

"See you in a little bit!" Leo called after them. Once they were a block away, Leo and Caroline looked at each other and burst into relieved laughter.

"I guess now we have to make JP a present," Leo said.

Caroline giggled, "Oh, darn, I have no choice."

"Ugh, don't be weird about it." Leo sighed. "I have enough terrible things happening already."

"Okay, okay. So what were you going to tell me?"

"I think it might be easier if I just show you," Leo said dramatically, watching the shadows of leaves on the sidewalk. She reached for the feeling of slipping into them, wrapping herself in the veil between worlds that Caroline had first showed her with her spell months ago. She closed her eyes and let out a deep breath, just like she'd practiced this morning.

"Uh . . . is the idea to just sit here doing nothing?" Caroline said.

Leo's eyes shot open, and she frowned. She was still visible. The sun was so warm and the day so lovely, and the excitement of showing off her power made her stomach light and bubbly instead of heavy. She tried again, scrunching her eyes closed and clenching her fists, but the feeling she had so easily conjured this morning was nowhere to be found, and Caroline shifted on the curb next to her, probably confused and maybe even bored and annoyed.

Leo tried to feel sad that she was letting her friend down—sadness seemed to be the missing ingredient she needed to turn invisible—but it was like trying to tickle yourself; her brain just couldn't fall for its own trick.

"So," Caroline said finally. "Is this supposed to be a magic thing? Do you want me to help?"

"No, it's—I mean yes, but I shouldn't need any help," Leo said, her voice dangerously close to a whine. "I was trying to show you my birth-order power, except I . . . I guess I can't do it on command." She crossed her arms and huffed, feeling childish and powerless. Usually when someone told her she couldn't do something, she would try even harder to do it. But she wasn't sure what to do when the person limiting her was herself.

"Your birth-order power? What is it?"

"Invisibility," Leo replied. "It kind of comes and goes, but this morning I was—"

"Wait, invisibility?" Caroline's ear-to-ear grin didn't match Leo's mood. "That's so cool! How long have you known? Is it fun? Can you still touch things when you've disappeared? Have you spied on anyone yet?"

Despite her frustration, Leo smiled as she caught some of Caroline's contagious excitement. "It wasn't that fun," she said, "because I didn't know how it happened at first. But yeah, I guess I did do a little spying."

"No way! On who?"

"Um." Leo squirmed a bit. "You and Brent and JP, at the library. Sorry."

"That's. So. Cool!" Caroline's eyes were wide. "I mean, it would be great if you could promise not to spy on me without permission anymore? That's a little bit creepy. But it's still amazing."

"I promise," Leo said with a laugh. "It was an accident anyway. I mostly just saw you playing Catan."

"Even worse," Caroline said, face serious. "Now you'll know all my secret strategies."

"I turn invisible; I don't read minds." Leo laughed again. "Your secrets are safe unless you write them on your palm and don't know that I'm behind you."

Caroline laughed too. "So cool." The two girls sat in silence for a moment. "So why can't you control it?"

"I don't know!" Leo groaned. "It's only worked so far when I'm sad, which is why I'm having so much trouble. I mean, nobody else's birth-order magic depends on their feel—" Leo's mouth dropped open midsentence. "Oh. Except . . ."

Caroline nodded in understanding. "I guess we're going to have to talk to Isabel."

CHAPTER 13
UNEXPECTED ALLY

"Please don't tell Mamá yet," Leo begged her oldest sister. "I just want to understand what I'm doing first."

Standing in the office in front of the door Leo had closed behind her, Isabel was teary eyed and beaming. "But Leo, you're coming into your birth-order power! This is a huge moment that everyone should celebrate!"

"We can celebrate eventually," Leo said, "but I don't even know if I have it right yet. It only worked once."

"That's perfectly normal," Isabel assured her.

"Mine was a little spotty for the first couple of months too."

Months? Leo's eyebrows shot up. She didn't have months to get a handle on her powers. The bakery could be closed by then.

"Leo came to you because she knew you would understand," Caroline said sweetly. "She's so lucky to have older sisters to help her through all these confusing things."

Isabel softened at Caroline's charm. "All right, Little Leo, I'll keep your secret for now. So, what do you need from me?"

Leo slumped into Daddy's desk chair in relief. "You know how you have the power to control people's emotions? Do you ever have to be feeling a certain emotion yourself in order to make others feel it?"

Isabel's mouth quirked into the same smile she got when Leo asked her for help with her social studies homework—the smile that meant she was about to launch into a lecture. "Actually, I don't control emotions, exactly. That's how you perceive it, of course, but I'm really influencing . . . I guess you could call it your *aura*. I feel the energy around people, including myself, and then I can change the way the energy is moving, and that's what makes you feel different."

Leo didn't exactly see how that was different from controlling people's emotions, but she shrugged and nodded.

"As for needing to feel a certain emotion to use it . . . I don't anymore, but I think when I first started out I could only really use my power when I was very angry. So, fights with Marisol, mostly. I'd get angry, and then I'd accidentally make her angry, which would make me more angry . . . you get the idea. I didn't really know what I was doing or how I was doing it, and I couldn't tell her about my powers yet anyway." Isabel sighed. "When she found out, she didn't talk to me for a week. Another strike against magic in her book."

"So how did you learn to use it properly?" Leo asked. "When you were calm?"

"Just practice, I guess," Isabel said. "And time."

"But I don't have time!"

"What's wrong?" Isabel put on a frown borrowed straight from Mamá. "You just have to be patient."

"I can't be patient when Abuelo Logroño is scheming to close down the bakery and destroy our magic!"

Caroline and Isabel both reeled back. "Leo, are you serious?" her sister asked. "He told you this?"

Leo nodded.

"Well, you have to tell Mamá."

"She already knows." Bitterness stung Leo's throat. "The landlord is raising the rent on the bakery, and there's going to be competition from Honeybees—the bakery is in serious trouble, and she isn't even telling us anything about it. But I know Abuelo has something to do with it, and if we're going to fight back, we have to do it on our own. So please, Isabel, can you help make me sad so I can use my powers?"

Isabel shook her head. "I don't think that's a good idea, Leo."

Leo's heart sank down to her toes. Her family was impossible. Did they want to sit here and do nothing and let the bakery—let the magic—fail? Why wouldn't they trust her, or at least help her?

"Leo," Caroline whispered. "Leo!"

"What?"

"I think you're doing it."

Leo looked down at her arms. Sure enough, they sparkled and swirled in and out of sight. Leo clapped, and the magic faded away.

"Wow," Isabel whispered. "That's . . . very interesting. I can't wait to see you once you get the hang of it."

"So you'll help?" Leo asked.

Isabel took a long breath. "I would love to

experiment with you. I don't know about all the rest of it."

"Isabel," Leo wheedled, "I just want to gather information. I have a plan. I just need to be sad."

"I'm sorry, Leo," Isabel said. "I don't think I'm suited for this."

"But—" Caroline began.

Isabel stopped her with an outstretched hand. "What I mean is, my influence doesn't last long enough for you to do any real sneaking or spying. It would be better to use something more portable, like an herb pouch."

Leo's discouraged frown twisted into a grin as Isabel winked at her.

"I know you, Leo. If you say you have a plan to fix a problem, it's a safe bet. Plus, if everything Mamá said about our abuelo is true, I'd like to make sure we have a few tricks up our sleeve, something that gives us the upper hand."

"An herb pouch . . ." Leo considered. "What would I do with it?"

"There are different varieties, but I was thinking you could put pinches of herb on your tongue to get the effect. We're so used to eating our spells. And I don't know if chasing sadness is the answer. We want you to move beyond your power being tied to an emotion. Maybe cinnamon to give you more strength, or something to give balance and stability, or . . ."

"Acónito!" Caroline piped up. "Aconite, also called monkshood. It's used for invisibility spells! I just finished memorizing it for my quiz before your aunt left."

"Perfect!" Leo leaped out of the chair with enough excitement to send it spinning.

"Hold on." Isabel held out a hand. "Aconite or monkshood, also called *wolfsbane*. Wolfsbane is one of the most toxic plants in the world. I wouldn't want Leo touching that, let alone eating it."

"Oops." Caroline's eyes grew wide. "I guess I should review that packet one more time."

"It was a good thought," Isabel murmured. "Feminine energy, protection, invisibility. Maybe we could use it in a different type of spell . . . a candle or something, except you can't really carry a lit candle with you while you're sneaking around, and it would have a time limit, and that's not great for—what are you planning again?"

Leo knew exactly where she wanted to start. "I'm going to spy on Belinda O'Rourke, the lady who's opening Honeybees and trying to put us out of business. I have a hunch she's working with Abuelo, but I need proof if Mamá is going to believe me."

"Why do you think Abuelo is trying to sabotage

the bakery?" Isabel asked. "I know he's been a terrible dad and grandfather, but he's never tried to hurt any of us. Why now?"

"Because now he knows there's a powerful Logroño he can train," came a voice. "And he'll do anything to get his hands on her."

Isabel jumped away from the door as it cracked open, and Caroline jumped when JP's face appeared in the crack. Leo was too stunned by his words to move at all.

"Shh!" she hissed. "Get in here!" She ran to the door to pull JP inside and found Brent standing behind him wringing his hands.

"It's my fault," he admitted. "I mentioned your grandpa, and it turns out JP actually knows he's a brujo, and so he sort of put the pieces together himself. It turns out he didn't need to be kept in the dark at all, and he might be able to help. So . . . you're welcome?"

"Just come inside." Leo sighed, too confused to be all that annoyed. She had never told Brent the details about Abuelo's magic training, so how could he blab a secret he didn't know himself?

The office was getting crowded now, and Leo worried that Mamá or Daddy would come to investigate at any moment.

"How do you know that Abuelo Logroño wants to train me?" she asked JP.

"He wants to train you?" Isabel asked. "In what?"

"Turning invisible," Leo said. "And I guess some other stuff, like fighting evil magical creatures or something?"

"Yup, he tried the same thing on me," JP answered. "He was all 'You're very special, Juan Pablo Logroño. . . .' Nobody even calls me that unless I'm in trouble."

"And he wants me to be a saltasombras, like him," Leo added.

"A salta *what?*" Brent asked. Standing in the middle of the office, his head bounced left and right to follow the different speakers like a video-game character glitching. "Do you have salt magic now too?"

"It means a shadow jumper," Caroline explained, pulling Brent to the corner. "She can disappear. But she can't control it yet."

"You're a saltasombras?" Leo asked JP. "Why didn't you tell me?"

"I'm not." JP shook his head. "Abuelo tested me; I guess I didn't have enough magic. He was really upset because I made it through the first spell—a memory spell, something that makes people forget things. Which is further than anyone else had gotten, I guess. But then he said a whole bunch of weird things about me getting my Logroño name from my mom instead of having my dad's name. . . ." JP inspected the zipper of his fanny pack. "It was really rude, actually. It didn't make me feel very good."

"He's like that," Leo said, patting her cousin on the arm. "That's why he's a bad guy."

"I still wish you had told us." Isabel tapped her finger against her lip and squinted. "When did this happen?"

"A little over a year ago," JP said. "He said he didn't bother with me before because I was just raised by my mom? I guess he's getting desperate for someone to train."

"What's wrong with having a single mom?" Brent growled from the corner.

Isabel nodded. "That explains why he decided it was worth it to face us. I wonder if that means he's been revealing himself to all the cousins. We always assumed it was just us because of our mom's magic."

"Right, so about that." JP held up a finger. "Are you saying you have a whole different set of magical powers? Why didn't Alma and Belén tell me? Why didn't any of you?"

"Well, we kind of did," Leo said. "At your mom's party."

"The baking?" JP said. "I thought that was a joke!"

"So he was focusing on Leo's family," Caroline said. "But then your mom warded him away, right? I'm guessing he gave up until he was sure he had no other options."

"How do you know so much about this?" Brent asked Caroline. "How does everyone know so much about this?"

"You're right," Leo said, ignoring Brent. "I've talked with Abuelo Logroño. I know what he wants and what he's doing. Our protective spells are supposed to stop thieves from entering the bakery— which means he must have had help to steal the mixing bowl. We need to find his accomplice. I think it's Belinda O'Rourke, but whether it's her or someone else, Mamá won't believe me. Unless I find proof." She looked around the small room. "If we don't stop him, he's going to take Amor y Azúcar down. So does that catch everyone up? Can we get started?"

"We haven't solved the problem of your power yet," Isabel reminded her. "We can't put aconite in an herb pouch for you. If only there was another herb with the same properties, one that you could consume without getting sick. . . ."

Leo opened her mouth to ask about different ways to look at the problem, but Isabel's phrasing sparked something for her. *Another herb with the same properties.*

"Spice magic!" she cried. "Isabel, we can do that with spice magic!"

"Shh!" Caroline glanced at the door, and they all held their breath for a moment. When they heard no footsteps, Isabel turned back to Leo, finger tapping her lips."Leo, that's perfect! I should have thought of it. It's been so long since I studied spice magic—it's an obscure branch of magic, since most spell casters don't create magic that's meant to be eaten."

Leo beamed. "So we can make that herb pouch to help me stay invisible. In the meantime"—she turned to JP, Brent, and Caroline—"would y'all be willing to do some reconnaissance work?"

"Anything to save my adopted bruja family," Caroline whispered with a smile.

"If it means getting some revenge on the world's worst grandpa, I'm down," JP said.

"I have no idea what's going on." Brent shrugged. "But you can always count on me. As long as I have clear instructions, and competent partners to help me out, and something to make sure I don't get hungry while we're on the job."

Leo laughed. "Actually, I think you'll be good at the observation part of this. Isn't that the first part of the scientific method?"

Brent perked up a little bit at that. "Can I use my scientific journal to take notes?" He pulled a palm-sized notebook out of his back pocket.

Leo beamed. "I was hoping you would."

CHAPTER 14
SPICE MAGIC

Brent, Caroline, and JP practiced their spy skills by exiting the bakery without anyone noticing—sneaking past Mamá while she was putting two giant cake pans in the oven for a lamb-shaped Easter cake, and waiting until Daddy was distracted by a customer to make a run for the front door. Leo had given them instructions for staking out the site of the future Honeybees Café and researching the O'Rourke family. Caroline was on magical component watch, keeping an eye out for candles, herbs, or symbols that would hint at brujería at work in the half-remodeled building. JP was in charge of searching for the mixing bowl, and any sign of Abuelo Logroño. Brent was in charge of note-taking.

The second part of the mission was to find out a way for Leo to spy on Belinda O'Rourke. That part might even be more important; Leo wasn't sure if the dark, dusty Honeybees building would hold many useful clues. But she didn't want to leave it unexamined. Besides, sending her friends ahead meant they could get the plan started while Leo cooked up a special spice-magic herb pouch with Isabel. Then she would be ready to act on their information.

"Mamá, are you good for another minute?" Isabel asked. "Leo wanted to practice spice magic, so I thought I could show her a few things."

Mamá looked up from dropping food coloring into dough for the top of Easter-egg-colored conchas. "What a good thing to practice! I'm so proud of you, Leo. Yes, I'll be fine here for a while. Go ahead."

Leo felt a twinge of guilt. Mamá thought that practicing spice magic would keep Leo out of Abuelo Logroño–flavored trouble, when really it was the opposite.

Marisol grumbled about doing all the work in the bakery, but when Leo tried to whisper in her older sister's ear to let her know about the plan, she held up a hand.

"I saw you hiding with all your friends, cucaracha. I know you're up to something. But I'm perfectly happy to keep the bakery running while you and Isabel mess with whatever magical mischief you've got cooking."

"I was going to tell you," Leo promised, afraid that Marisol might feel left out in spite of what she'd just said.

"Somehow I suspect I'll find out about it soon enough." Marisol gave her a teasing smile. "Try not to . . . I don't know, create any rifts in the space-time continuum or burn anything to the ground. Be careful."

Leo stuck out her tongue. "I always am."

Isabel climbed precariously onto a rolling chair to root the wolfsbane out of the highest cabinet in the least accessible corner of the office. Leo pulled down the molcajete. Lastly, Isabel fetched a mostly empty bag of sugar.

"Sugar is one of the most basic touchstones of our magic," she explained, rolling down the sides of the large paper bag to reach the white crystals at the bottom. "We have an affinity for it that stretches beyond its typical use in love and attraction spells." She lifted a handful out of the bag and let it run through her fingers. "For us, this is a magical blank canvas."

Leo nodded. If the spice magic was performed correctly, the sugar would take on the magical energy of the aconite without absorbing any of its toxicity. She let Isabel shake a few dried aconite flowers out of their paper bag and into the stone bowl, but when her sister reached for the tejolote to grind them down, Leo kept it gripped in her hand.

"It's better if I do it, right? Mamá showed me how."

"Oh . . ." Isabel hesitated. "It's just that—I'm afraid it could be dangerous."

"You can watch to make sure everything looks right," Leo said. "Please, Isabel? I can do this."

Isabel pushed the molcajete toward Leo. "Okay, go ahead."

Leo took a deep breath. Aconite wasn't simply poisonous—it had many dangerous characteristics that had earned it ominous nicknames like wolfsbane. It could be used to hurt magic users, to halt change and growth, to obscure the truth of things. In short, it sounded like an herb Abuelo Logroño would love. It was even rumored to hurt werewolves, hence the name—hadn't Abuelo listed shape-shifters among his threatening magical creatures?

And along with all its sinister uses, aconite could also make things invisible. The thought made Leo uneasy, a reminder that her invisibility wasn't just a normal birth-order power from Mamá's family magic. It also came from her Logroño family, a legacy tainted by Abuelo Logroño's ugly way of treating others, including his own family. Was her invisibility proof that she belonged to that legacy?

As she made circles around the molcajete, thirteen times clockwise and seven times counterclockwise, Leo tried to focus on the purpose of the spice magic. She wanted to control her invisibility. She wanted to help her family and the bakery. The repetitive motion helped to slow her pounding pulse. When she was finished, she poured the aconite powder carefully into a plastic baggie Isabel held open, then sealed it up and dropped it into the small wire trash can under the desk, hopefully leaving its power behind in the molcajete.

"Now, the sugar," Isabel prompted.

Leo nodded, tilting and shaking the bag until she could scoop out a handful big enough to cover the bottom of the molcajete. The sugar cascaded out of her hand, and she licked a cluster of clinging crystals off her thumb, the sweet burst clear and calming. She worked so often with dough and batter and herbs and recipes that she sometimes lost track of the base of her family's kitchen brujería. Amor y Azúcar, the two things that her bisabuela's bisabuela had used in every spell she wrote for her daughters. The name of the bakery that bound their power together through the generations. This was Leo's inheritance, just as much as the Logroño name. The sugar made a soft crunch against the stone bowl, turning the toxic strength of the aconite into a safer and sweeter magic.

Leo's nose tickled with the smell of magic, and for the first time since Abuelo's appearance, she felt sure of herself. She finished her thirteenth circle, then set down the tejolote.

"Great," Isabel said. "Now I just want to run a few quick tests. . . ."

Leo was so caught up in the feeling of the magic, she had already licked her finger, dipped it into the fine white powder, and pressed it to her tongue before she registered what Isabel was saying.

Her stomach dropped like she was on a roller coaster and the hair on the back of her neck prickled, and she wondered for a moment what the symptoms of aconite poisoning were, if there was an antidote . . . and a second later she felt the familiar brush of cold against her skin.

"Leo!" Isabel whispered in an angry, muffled tone. "You have to be careful!" Her eyes flashed around the room, and Leo smiled as she realized that Isabel couldn't see her.

"Leo . . . ?" Isabel's whisper took on a tinge of

anxiety. "You are here, right?"

"Hi, Isabel," Leo tested, but her sister couldn't hear her either. She tried tapping on the desk in front of her. "Can you hear that?"

"Leo?" Isabel asked. "Can you say something?" Her voice was louder, making it easier to hear past the muffle of the veil. Leo tried knocking on the desk again, harder this time.

Isabel cocked her head. "Was that you?"

Leo knocked again.

"That's weird," Isabel whispered. "I hear it, but it sounds really far away, like an echo or something."

Leo reached for the rolling chair in front of the desk and pushed it hard into the desk. The crash sounded muffled in Leo's ears, but Isabel jumped and a stack of papers fell to the floor.

"Okay then," Isabel said, rolling her eyes while she and Leo both stacked the papers back up. "So you can't make sounds yourself, but you can interact with objects."

Leo drummed on the desk in response. *Dum-dum-da-dum-dum.*

"You could just do once for yes and twice for no," Isabel said.

Leo snuck behind her sister and tugged the end of her braid twice.

Isabel spun around, eyes narrowed. "Very funny, Leo," she grumped, glaring a foot to the right of where Leo actually stood.

The sting of cold, the triumph of a spell that worked perfectly right on the first try, and the look on Isabel's face combined to make Leo start laughing. She laughed until her face was warm and her arms prickled with pins and needles like they had just fallen asleep. Slowly, Isabel turned her head and scanned the space, her eyes eventually finding Leo.

"So laughing brings you back," she noted. "That's convenient."

"It worked!" Leo jumped and pumped her fist. "We did it!"

Isabel nodded, tapping her bottom lip. "Yes, but don't run off on a spy mission just yet. I'd like to see how long a pinch of this lasts when you don't break it by laughing."

"Time for another test!" Leo reached for the molcajete, grabbing a pinch of powder. Before her sister could say anything, Leo stuck out her tongue and disappeared.

The invisibility powder lasted approximately eight minutes per taste, which felt like an eternity when

Leo was sitting in the office with nothing to do, but would probably feel very short when she was spying. Eating a bigger or smaller pinch didn't make a difference, but eating a new pinch restarted the timer. While Leo could break the spell with laughter, she couldn't find a way to extend it, no matter how much she tried to conjure the feelings of fear and sadness she had felt yesterday.

Isabel gave her a ravioli-sized leather pouch to hang around her neck, filled with the rest of the spelled sugar powder. Once Leo had helped Isabel frost the rest of the Easter cake orders, she borrowed her sister's phone and texted Caroline.

JP, Brent, and Caroline tumbled back into the bakery with much less stealth than they had used when they left. They were all laughing about something Brent had written in his notebook, and after getting permission to eat a snack, they ran into the back of the bakery, scattering crumbs. Mamá sighed, Marisol rolled her eyes, and Leo wondered if she could use her new invisibility powder on other people.

"Come on." She ushered everyone into the office. "Did you find anything?"

"We found lots of things," Brent said through a mouthful of pastry, flipping his notebook open and holding out a list that almost covered the page. Leo's heart swelled with hope.

"But nothing useful," Caroline clarified, glaring at Brent. "At least, I don't think so. Sorry, Leo."

"I still think we should have jumped the fence," JP grumbled. "The new windows weren't even installed yet. We could have gone inside. I bet we would have found something."

Leo grabbed the notebook from Brent's hand so she could see it more clearly. The list was mostly a catalog of all the insects and different types of litter he'd spotted. Brent had also done a sketch of the Honeybees logo, just as cutesy as it had looked on the website.

"So there was nothing suspicious at all?" Leo asked.

JP shook his head. "It's still a work site. Inside they're putting in all new ovens and counters, so the O'Rourkes probably don't even spend much time there yet."

Leo nodded slowly. "That's fine," she said. "The house was always going to be a better chance. How did that part of the mission go?"

"Great!" Brent said. "JP is awesome at stalking people online!"

"I'm not," JP protested, face flushing. "I just found Belinda O'Rourke's daughter, Becky, on social media. She posted a picture of the new house. Brent's the one who recognized the street."

Leo nodded. "Great. Isabel made up a welcome gift, all ready to deliver." She pointed to a cardboard bakery box filled with pan dulce and tied with a ribbon. "Are you ready?"

Brent stuffed the last quarter of his ojo de buey into his mouth. "I wath *bown* weady!" He gulped and cleared his throat. "Wait, what are we doing again?"

"*You* are going to go welcome a new family into town," Leo said, handing him the gift box. "*I* am going to do something sneaky."

CHAPTER 15
THE O'ROURKES

"So your invisibility basically works like my diabetes," JP said as they turned onto the street where Brent was "eighty-five percent sure" the O'Rourke house would be. "You have to take invisibility powder to stay invisible, I have to take insulin to stay alive. More or less the same deal."

"I think this is it!" Brent said. "Wait . . ." He turned from the house he was pointing at to the house across the street. "I think *that* is it!"

The O'Rourkes' new house was walking distance from the bakery, just a few blocks from Caroline and Brent's street. It was the kind of house Mamá dreamed of: two stories, brick, with white trim decorating the windows and foggy glass patterning the front door. Leo checked JP's phone, where Becky O'Rourke's post showed a short looping video of a big black dog running around the same front yard they were looking at now, ears flopping and tongue lolling.

"Moved in just in time for spring," the caption read. "Bumble is excited."

Leo frowned. It was hard to feel like a spy staking out villains when the villains had adorable fluffy pets. Then she shook her head. She couldn't get distracted from her mission.

"Everyone clear on the plan?" Caroline asked.

"You've gone over it five times," Brent said. "I promise, I'll stay totally focused."

"And if not, I'll accidentally crash into him or something," JP assured her.

"Why does everybody resort to violence with me?" Brent asked.

JP shrugged. "I've known you for like three days, and I can already tell it's sometimes the only way to get you to stop talking." He patted Brent's arm apologetically, making the shorter boy blush.

"Just stick to Caroline's plan, and everything will go perfectly," Leo said before the teasing could continue. "Don't forget that I'll signal if I need help, but it can be hard to hear, so keep an ear out."

"We've got it." Caroline pushed her bangs out of her eyes and squared her shoulders. "Let's go."

Leo loosened the top of the leather pouch hanging from her neck. Caroline leaned forward and sniffed. Brent, whose last experience with magic had exploded dramatically, covered his ears and scrunched his eyes closed. JP watched, eyes wide and eyebrows raised.

"Sorry you got kind of thrown in the middle of all this," she told her cousin. "We would have shown you our magic eventually, probably. But it's hard to know how to bring it up, and it has to stay sort of secret. So, you know, no social media posts."

"I get it," JP said. "I'm just a little . . . I don't know," He rubbed the back of his neck. "It was frustrating when Abuelo Logroño showed up just to tell me that magic was real but I didn't have any. It was like, I'd been waiting my whole life for something like that, and I blew it. Like I was one of those extra characters in DragonBlood instead of a friend of dragons."

"Finally," Brent said, "somebody gets it."

"Sorry," JP said. "It's not cool to be jealous."

Leo was too baffled to say anything. JP was jealous? JP, who always knew the right joke to tell, who was so good-looking that her friends got all flustered around him, who already felt like a core part of their group? JP was jealous of *her*? "But you're so cool!" she blurted out.

Caroline and Brent nodded until Caroline caught herself and pretended to be examining her ring.

JP smiled. "I didn't mean to fish for that compliment, but thanks. I guess I must be pretty cool, considering how cool my cousins are."

Leo smiled back. She nodded at her friends. Then she popped a pinch of invisibility powder onto her tongue. With a feeling of jumping off a diving board into ice-cold water, her power took effect.

"That. Is. Wild," Brent whispered, waving his hand out in front of him and hitting Leo's shoulder. "Aaah! Is that you? Weird!"

"Okay, okay, stick to the plan," Caroline whispered. She breathed in deeply before taking determined steps up the front walkway to the O'Rourkes' door. Balancing the bakery box on one hand, she rang the doorbell, then took three steps back, just like they had learned doing cookie sales as Brownies. (Mamá had a soft spot for Thin Mints in spite of her general ban on factory-produced baked goods.)

A bark sounded from inside. Leo squeezed up the front steps to stand right behind Caroline, close enough to hear a muffled voice trying to hush the protective dog.

"Mom, can you come down here? There's someone at the— Never mind, I've got it."

The lock clicked and the door cracked open, revealing a pale freckled face and one brown eye. "Um, hi, sorry." The girl, who looked about Leo's age, put her hand down to catch a black dog. "Let me just—" Becky O'Rourke gave the dog a gentle shove backward and then slipped out the door and slammed it behind her.

"Hi," she said again, brushing wispy strands of dark brown hair from her forehead and straightening her T-shirt that showed a cartoon beach. "Can I help you?"

Caroline cleared her throat, glancing over her shoulder at an empty space nowhere near where Leo actually stood. The plan for Leo to slip through the open door while Caroline talked was already a failure. Leo clenched her fists in frustration. Cats didn't need to be restrained from attacking visitors. Well, most of the time.

Caroline straightened up and held the bakery box out in front of her. "I'm Caroline Campbell. I live in the neighborhood. We brought you some snacks to say welcome."

"Oh, thank you." Becky smiled and tucked her hair behind her ear. "All of you."

The boys, who had been standing frozen, jerked into motion with belated smiles and waves.

"I don't live here," JP said. Not exactly an enthusiastic introduction.

"I'm Brent?" Brent squeaked, which was somehow even worse. Leo buried her face in her hands.

"Sorry about them," Caroline said. "Brent lives next door to me. And JP is visiting his cousins for spring break. More importantly, however: we brought conchas and puerquitos!"

"Oh, are those . . ." Becky reached for the box, "Are those cookies?"

Leo's eyes nearly rolled out of her head. How could the O'Rourkes pretend to compete with Amor y Azúcar's selection of pan dulce when they didn't even recognize the names?

"There's also flan!" Brent said, "In case you're gluten intolerant. Are you gluten intolerant? My sister gets terrible diarrhea whenever she eats anything made with wheat, plus she would eventually get cancer or something."

Becky glanced at Caroline, who threw up her hands with another apologetic shrug.

"Right," Becky said. "We tried eating gluten free a few years ago—it was one of my mom's phases. But we didn't notice any difference. Um, I hope your sister is okay. Thanks for all this."

There was a stretched silence. Becky put her hand on the doorknob.

"I have type one diabetes!" JP half shouted.

Leo was learning that her cousin, like Brent, did not have the makings of a great spy, or even a good accomplice.

"It's a common misconception that you get diabetes from eating sugar," JP continued. "It's actually autoimmune, like celiac disease."

"And asthma." Brent nodded solemnly. "Your body thinks it's fighting bad germs, but really it's just attacking itself."

Leo marched between the babbling boys and poked a finger straight into each of their shoulders. *Stop talking.*

"Well . . . ," Becky said. "That's . . . interesting. Nice to meet all of you." Whining and scratching noises were coming from the other side of the front door. "I'd better get back to Bumble."

No! Leo reached out an invisible hand, feeling totally helpless. If Becky snuck back inside without fully opening the door, she'd never be able to follow.

"Can I use your bathroom?" Caroline said, breathless and frantic. "Sorry, I, uh, really have to go."

Leo could have kissed her quick-thinking friend.

"I thought you lived here?" Becky asked, gesturing down the block.

"No, yeah, I do. I just . . . well, I live a couple streets down actually, and across Pine Lane. But . . . my toilet is broken."

Becky looked at Caroline. Caroline looked back at Becky. Leo wondered if she could get into the house by smashing one of the big picture windows.

"It's been a long day," Caroline said, her tiny smile putting a matching smile on Becky's lips. "I've been stuck babysitting these ones for a couple days now."

JP and Brent started to protest, but Leo pinched them.

"Yeah, makes sense." Becky giggled. "Come on in. Do all of you go to the middle school here?"

She turned the doorknob, caught Bumble's collar, and pulled the dog inside, leaving the door open for the rest of them.

Adding an extra pinch of invisibility powder to her tongue just to be safe, Leo slipped in behind her.

CHAPTER 16
SNEAKY SPY STUFF

"I'm going to be starting in seventh grade next year," Becky explained as the others entered the house. "But since we moved so late in the year my old school is letting me take all my final exams online. Bathroom's over there." She pointed Caroline to a door just inside the front hallway. With the front door closed, she released her grip on Bumble, who ran in a circle sniffing and jumping on the guests.

"Thanks," Caroline said. "That's cool that you get kind of a long vacation, huh?"

"I guess." Becky brushed hair out of her face. "I just did it because it stinks to have to start new classes in the middle of the year. On top of moving."

Caroline nodded. "I've, uh, done that. But hey, starting next year you'll be in class with me and Brent, so that will be good."

Leo made a face. Becky O'Rourke wouldn't be in her class if she could help it. If things went according to plan, she would send the O'Rourkes running back to their California beaches faster than they could say "concha." Becky didn't even want to be in Rose Hill anyway. Really, Leo was doing her a favor.

JP chimed in with his story about moving schools, told at an appropriate volume and with no mention of diarrhea, so maybe he was warming up to the mission. Leo left the group to sneak down the hall. The entryway of the house already looked beautifully decorated, with a fancy rug and metal flowers positioned next to a bright red painting on the wall. To the left, a chandelier hung over an empty room with a fireplace. To the right, a flight of stairs curved upward, dark wooden steps gleaming. And straight ahead, Leo caught a glimpse through a doorway of stainless steel and tile.

In the Logroño house, the kitchen was the best place to find what you were looking for, whether it was important papers, a missing sister, or a delicious breakfast. Leo strode down the hall, ready to investigate.

A low growl stopped her in her tracks. She turned to see Bumble with her tail down and lip curled, standing about two feet behind her and sniffing the air between growls. Becky, Caroline, JP, and Brent all followed the dog's gaze. Leo clenched her fists, hoping her invisibility powder was holding up.

"Sorry, she's weird about the new house sometimes," Becky said. "Hey, didn't you need the bathroom?"

"Oh, yeah, of course!" Caroline laughed. "Um, but finish your story first."

Leo backed slowly away from Bumble—she was pretty sure the dog couldn't see her, but she wasn't convinced she wouldn't attack by smell alone—and ducked into the kitchen. It was a disappointing jumble of cardboard boxes and dirty dishes. Leo peeked into the half-unpacked boxes, moving slowly because she wasn't totally sure what would happen if she picked up an object and held it. Would it disappear too, or would it look like it was floating? Deciding it was better safe than sorry, Leo left things where they were, but checked each box carefully without removing its contents.

She found fancy pots and pans and spatulas without the scratches and stains that would hint at a family of bakers, and no stolen mixing bowl. She opened each of the kitchen's many cabinets as well, but they were empty. The only things on the shiny black stone counter were a fancy teapot and an electric kettle, surrounded by three squeeze bottles of honey with different shapes and labels.

"Becky?" A voice echoed from somewhere above them. "Is someone there?"

"Yeah, Mom, it's some neighbors."

Leo peeked into the hallway and followed Becky's eyes up to a second-floor balcony overlooking the entryway. Belinda O'Rourke leaned over the railing with a smartphone pressed to her ear and a matching tablet cradled in her arm. Unlike her picture in the *Rose Hill Chronicle*, she wasn't perfectly made up or dressed in a jacket that made her look like a TV lawyer. Instead, her dark brown curls spilled out of a bun on the top of her head to frame a face as freckled as Becky's.

"Hello there." She pulled the phone away from her mouth as she spoke, waving it at Brent and JP. "So you boys live nearby? Don't tell me I'm going to have to chase you away from my beautiful daughter!" She laughed, then tapped her tablet violently.

"Mom," Becky groaned.

"Well, I imagine these guys must have caught sight of you—otherwise they wouldn't have thought to welcome you to the neighborhood, am I right?"

JP scratched his earlobe and fiddled with his fanny-pack zipper. Brent mumbled something unintelligible.

"Mom, cut it out," Becky sighed.

Caroline emerged from the bathroom. "Oh, hello." She looked up. "You must be Mrs. O'Rourke. Pleased to meet you. Welcome to the neighborhood."

"Oh, so this young lady came up with the welcoming idea." Mrs. O'Rourke smiled down at Caroline. "Isn't that sweet? That makes more sense."

Caroline's eyes darted to Becky, who just shrugged. Brent looked at JP, eyebrows raised.

"Well, thank you so much for thinking of us," Mrs. O'Rourke continued, reminding Leo of Abuelo Logroño with the way she didn't notice or care how her words were received.

"No problem," Caroline said.

"I have a lot of work to get done, but please stay awhile—we have drinks in the kitchen. I want Becky to have friends and fit in here." Mrs. O'Rourke tapped her tablet again, brought her phone back to her ear, and wandered away from the balcony edge and out of sight.

"I had friends in California," Becky muttered.

"Your mom seems . . . really busy," Caroline said. "Does she work from home?"

Leo smiled. Caroline really was the best accomplice, asking questions to get Becky talking about her mom.

"Yeah, for now," Becky said. "She's starting a business. A café. She's always in her office."

Leo glanced back at the balcony. The office must be up there.

"Oh, I think I've seen that sign," Caroline said. "What was it called?"

Leo backed up as Becky led Caroline, Brent, and JP into the kitchen, then ducked out before the door could swing shut. She made a beeline for the stairs, remembering to take another pinch of invisibility powder before climbing the first step.

Upstairs wasn't as neatly decorated as the entryway. More cardboard boxes covered a couch and table in the landing. In the first room Leo peeked into, the carpet still had the indentations of old furniture, and it smelled like fresh paint. It was empty except for a box full of beige sheets and towels, and not a mixing bowl to be seen.

Taped to the door of the next room was a poster collage of pictures of Becky with kids who must've been her California friends. In the spaces between the photos, rainbow letters spelled out MISS YOU ALREADY!

Leo frowned, guilt freezing her hand on Becky's bedroom doorknob.

She should check the office first. It was a more likely place to hide heirlooms stolen from a rival business. She crept across the landing, rubbing the goose bumps on her arms for reassurance that she was still invisible. A floorboard creaked as she stepped on it, and she froze as Bumble's growling started again.

"Shh, hey girl, settle down."

The click of Bumble's claws traveled up the stairs, and Leo held still as the dog bounded onto the landing with her teeth showing. *Cats are better,* Leo thought spitefully as Bumble surveyed the room, sniffing the air and growling.

"I'm sorry." Becky's voice carried from downstairs. "She's been so weird since we moved here, always barking at nothing."

When Bumble didn't find anything, she trotted to a cracked door and nosed it open. Leo caught a glimpse of Belinda O'Rourke's knee in a fancy leather desk chair.

Before she could lose courage or the door could swing shut, Leo followed the dog straight into the office.

"What are you bothering me for?" Mrs. O'Rourke asked Bumble, who was pawing at her leg and whining. She pushed the dog down gently and looked up, sending a lightning bolt of panic through Leo's heart as her eyes seemed to fall right where she stood. But she looked away just as quickly.

"Work, work, work," she said in goofy low-pitched baby talk. "All you do now is work all the time. You never play with me."

Mrs. O'Rourke was pretending to be Bumble and talking to herself. Dog people were so weird.

"I know, girl," Mrs. O'Rourke answered in her normal voice. "I'm sorry. But this business is important. It's important for us to be here for Becky. It has nothing to do with *him*, I promise. Now, go downstairs, girl. I bet Becky will give you a treat."

Bumble's ears perked up at the last word, but she stopped in the doorway, sniffing the space around Leo's shoes and whining. Leo took tiny sidesteps until she wasn't blocking the way, and Bumble eventually slipped out the door.

Leo scanned the office inch by inch, trying to pick out possible hiding spots. Mrs. O'Rourke was a weirdo dog owner, and she had basically confessed right in front of Leo. "It has nothing to do with *him*," Mrs. O'Rourke had said, which meant that it absolutely had everything to do with *him*, and Leo had no doubts that "him" meant Abuelo Logroño.

She had her proof. Now she just needed to find the mixing bowl.

But the office didn't offer many promising hiding spots. The bookshelves were still mostly empty, the desk made with thin bars of metal, modern and drawerless. Besides a laptop to match her phone and tablet, Mrs. O'Rourke didn't seem to need much equipment or storage space in her office. Leo half wanted to check all the shelves for hidden doors, but it seemed impractical to do it while Mrs. O'Rourke was sitting at her desk. Besides, the family had been in the house for only a week, hardly long enough for elaborate secret-door construction projects.

Leo checked the two bedrooms upstairs as quickly as she could without sacrificing thoroughness. She still felt a tiny bit bad poking her head into the corners of Becky's closet or checking under Mrs. O'Rourke's bathroom sink, but she pushed aside those feelings and focused instead on Mrs. O'Rourke's undeniable guilt. It wasn't nice to spy, but Leo would do anything to protect her family.

She was holding Becky's doorknob to keep it from clicking closed when she heard Caroline's voice, overly loud and echoing up from the first floor.

"Thanks so much for the tea. We should get going. Tell your mom thanks for having us. In fact, maybe I should go up and tell her myself that *we're leaving.*"

"Oh, that's not necessary," Becky said. Leo bit her lip. This would definitely be her best chance to leave the house without getting caught, and she knew Caroline was trying to send her a message. She didn't want to worry her friends by not showing up. But she hated to leave empty-handed. She was sure the O'Rourkes had the mixing bowl somewhere. She just needed more time to search!

"Well, I really hope to *see you soon.*" Caroline projected in her best reading-in-front-of-the-class voice. "We should *catch up.*"

Leo tugged at the pouch around her neck. She wanted to stay, but she couldn't abandon her accomplices.

She scrambled downstairs in time for another round of goodbyes. Leo thought that Caroline was going a bit overboard pretending to want Becky to call her up over the summer. But finally the front door opened, and Leo only had to shove JP out of the way a little bit so she could slip out.

The late-afternoon sun was bright, and Leo missed the feeling of its warmth on her face. This whole street was lined with tall oak trees that made a majestic line in the yards but, at this time of year, also covered the sidewalk in thick mats of orange-brown pollen.

"Okay." Caroline let out a big sigh when they reached the end of the block. "That went well, I think. Leo, you're here, right?"

As an answer, Leo kicked a pile of catkins, the dried pollen clusters exploding in a puff of dust. Brent covered his face, grumbling about allergies.

"Sorry," Leo said out loud, but of course no one could hear her. Instead she tried patting Brent's shoulder, but that just made him yelp and jump.

"How long until your powder wears off?" JP asked. "Or, wait, you can't answer that question. Shoot."

Leo stomped her foot, wishing for a birth-order power she could actually control. But the puff of pollen her foot kicked up gave her an idea. With a handful of catkins in each hand, she wiped clean a square of sidewalk with her foot. Then she sprinkled the catkins carefully to make a figure in the space.

"Is that a snake?" Brent asked.

"No, it's an S," Caroline said. "She's spelling something."

"I think it's supposed to be a five," JP guessed. "I did ask about how much time was left. I'm hoping that's minutes and not hours."

Leo tapped his shoulder excitedly.

"But we can speed it up, right?" Caroline asked. "We just have to make her laugh."

"Knock, knock," JP said with a wry smile.

"Who's there?" Brent replied immediately.

"Oh, um, I didn't actually have a knock-knock joke." JP tugged his fanny-pack zipper. "I just meant we should . . ."

"I have a great one," Caroline said, a glint in her eyes. "You start."

"Knock, knock," Brent said, smiling and helpful.

"Who's there?"

The pause stretched long as Caroline grinned expectantly at a totally confused and flustered Brent. "Hey, wait a second, that doesn't work!"

Leo giggled at the prank, but the laughter didn't reach her belly.

"Sorry, I tried." Caroline shrugged.

"It was a good joke," JP said.

"It's probably for the best," Brent muttered. "We don't want someone to look out their window and see Leo appear out of nowhere."

"Good point," said JP. "Let's walk while we wait."

Leo trailed along with her friends and her cousin, trying to think of something funny enough to break her spell despite Brent's worry. Everyone walked in silence, which just made her feel tense and curious.

Had her friends gathered any clues? Did their silence mean they hadn't learned anything? Nothing seemed very funny when she was stuck with a million questions and no way to answer them.

They reached Caroline and Brent's street just as Leo started to feel the warm pricks on her arms that meant the invisibility powder was wearing off. She rushed up to Caroline's porch so she would be slightly hidden as she appeared.

"There you are." Caroline smiled. "It's no fun not to be able to see you."

"Yeah, it's a little creepy," Brent added. "You got the creepiest power."

Leo glared at him until he dropped his eyes.

"Uh, I mean, it's probably useful, though. Did you find your bowl?"

"She obviously doesn't have the bowl with her, Brent." Caroline sighed. "She probably didn't find anything."

"But it would have been hard to carry it out the door without getting caught," JP argued. "Maybe she found it and now we have to plan a recovery mission."

"I can talk for myself now," Leo reminded them, "And no, I didn't find it. I was hoping maybe y'all had gotten some clues from Becky?"

"Oh." Caroline's eyes darted around the porch. "No. We were just talking about, you know, life and stuff."

"She didn't say anything about the move?" Leo asked. "She didn't mention, I don't know, a kind old stranger who gave her mom the idea to move?"

"Pretty much the opposite," JP said. "Her mom's been wanting to open Honeybees for a long time."

"Yeah, it seemed pretty normal," Brent said. "Nothing suspicious about it."

"I'm sorry, Leo." Caroline was staring at the floor now, twisting her ring around her finger. "I know you really thought they were the accomplices, but after talking to Becky . . . I think your mom might be right. It sounds like it's just normal nonmagical bad luck."

Leo felt like borrowing a page from Bumble's book and growling at her friend. "No way," she said. "Becky is lying. She has to be."

"I don't know why she would lie," Brent said.

"Because she obviously wouldn't admit that her family is only here to ruin my family's life," Leo snapped. "But we know that they are."

"It was a hunch," Caroline said with an infuriatingly sympathetic smile. "A reasonable hunch, but if you didn't find any proof . . ."

"I did find this in a drawer," Brent said, pulling a

crumpled paper out of his pocket. "I pretended to be looking for spoons. Clever, right?"

Leo snatched the paper from his hands. "What is it?" She smoothed the corners of the faded print image.

"An old Honeybees logo," Brent said "There's a date up in the corner. Five years ago. So Becky wasn't lying about that."

"Well, she's lying about something," Leo said. "Because I heard Mrs. O'Rourke say that she was really just here in town because of Abuelo Logroño!"

"You heard that?" JP asked. "She said those words exactly?"

"I . . . basically!" Leo frowned. "She talked about being here because of *him*. What else could that mean?"

"Just off the top of my head?" Caroline asked, rolling her eyes. "Could be a travel agent. Or a family member. Or someone she has a crush on. That's not exactly hard evidence." She sighed, easing the hardness out of her voice. "Becky . . . she's going through a hard time with the move, and she didn't even want to come here, and she misses her friends. If there was anything bad to say about Honeybees, she would have said it, but she didn't. I know it's hard for you to hear, but . . ."

Leo thought for a moment that her invisibility was simply wearing off, but the warmth spreading through her was just anger, not magic. "You think she's *nice*?" She spat the word at Caroline. "So, what, you're on her side after one conversation?"

"That's not what I'm . . . I'm not on anyone's side. I just—" Caroline looked to Brent for help. He traced the lines of the front porch with his toe but shifted his body, just a little, so that he stood with Caroline, the two of them facing Leo.

"Maybe you should talk to Becky," he said. "She was cool."

Leo looked at her friends. Together, they had fought messed-up spells, hunted spirits, plotted and planned, and played Catan. They had been through too much to not be on anyone's side. They were Leo's friends. They were supposed to be on Leo's side.

"You think Becky is cool?" Leo said. "Like you think JP is cool? You should really decide who you're in love with, Brent—it seems like a big problem for you."

"Leo," Caroline gasped while Brent's face flamed red. "What is wrong with you?"

Leo rounded on her other friend. "What's wrong is that my friends don't know how to be loyal."

Caroline's expression of outrage, disappointment, and hurt almost made Leo regret her words. She was tempted to turn invisible right then and there, but at the last second she remembered her cousin. "Come on, JP," she said. "Let's get out of here."

Her stomach tightened as she met his eyes. He looked uncomfortable, maybe even mad.

But whatever JP was feeling, he followed her off the front porch and onto the pollen-dusted sidewalk, to her relief.

"You've already learned a lot from your abuelo!" Caroline shouted behind her. "Like how to be cruel when you don't get your way!"

As she walked, Leo blinked blurry eyes and shivered, teetering on the edge of invisibility without using the powder. It felt like trying to balance a seesaw, or stay awake when she was falling asleep at the cash register on an early-morning shift.

"Uh, are you okay?" JP whispered. "You're sort of . . . winking."

Leo concentrated her thoughts, tipping the balance of the imaginary scale, holding her body on the normal side of the shadows, then letting go. Only when she was sure she was invisible did she look back over her shoulder to see Caroline's tears and Brent's angry glare.

She set her eyes forward and pushed herself back out of invisibility.

"I'm fine," she told JP, not even enjoying the fact that she had just taken control of her birth-order power. "Let's go."

CHAPTER 17
DISAPPEARING ACT

Leo kept her mind on the new feeling of balance. It kept her from seeing her friends' hurt faces or hearing Caroline's parting accusation. JP walked next to her in silence, body tense and still. Leo watched him out of the corner of her eye. He probably wished Alma and Belén were here so he wouldn't be stuck with Leo.

"Sorry," she said. "I didn't mean to . . . I'm sorry." Speaking broke her concentration, and her brain tipped back in the wrong direction. "Rats," she muttered, slipping out of invisibility.

"Hey, that's new," JP said. "I could hear you even when I couldn't see you."

"Really?" Leo's smile felt as precarious as her powers. "Maybe someday I'll be able to control that."

They turned onto Main Street. "You don't really need to apologize to me," JP said. "That was . . . rough. I know you're not *okay*, but, uh, are you okay?"

"The O'Rourkes are up to something," Leo said. "They stole our menu. They're trying to put us out of business. You believe me, right?"

JP sighed and stared at the blue sky. "I believe that there's definitely some shady business going on," he said. "I guess I'm just not sure that it's, you know, magically shady. Mrs. O'Rourke could just be a normal shady businessperson. Like Kingpin, or the Penguin. Or politicians."

"You don't think she's Abuelo's accomplice?" Leo asked.

JP fiddled with his fanny pack. "I don't know that much about our grandpa, but he doesn't seem to like single moms or woman-owned businesses or playing nice with anyone who doesn't share his last name."

Leo felt his words drop like stones in her belly, hard and cold and true. But if JP was right, that meant Leo was wrong, and Caroline and Brent . . .

They would hate her. They already hated her.

"Hang on." JP pulled his buzzing phone out of his pocket. "It's Uncle Luis. Um, what did we tell everyone again? We were going to Caroline's house?"

"Brent's," she corrected. "To play video games."

JP nodded, eyes widening nervously as he put the phone to his ear. "Hi, uh, we were just finishing playing Super—" He stopped to listen, which was probably for the best since his voice was too loud and stiff to sound honest. Leo waited, ready to snatch the phone away before be could say something that gave them all away.

"Mhm . . . um, okay, sure, here she is." JP handed the phone to Leo with a shrug.

"Hello?"

"Hi, Leonora." Daddy's voice was high with fake cheeriness. Leo's stomach clenched in preparation for more bad news. "We're just checking in to ask—and you're not in any trouble, we just need an honest answer, please—did you take the molcajete out of the bakery?"

"What? No! I left it right in the office!" Leo's heart lurched. "On your desk. Isabel saw me."

"Okay, okay." Daddy tried for soothing, but he still just sounded worried. "We had to check. Your mother's trying a scrying spell right now to see if she can get any answers. I'm sure it will . . . turn up. Enjoy your game."

Leo shook her head. "I'm coming to the bakery right now."

"You don't have to, Leonora. We have everything—"

"Stop it!" Leo slammed her finger on the red end-call button. "Stop lying, stop hiding things!" she shouted at the dark phone screen. "I know we're in trouble, I know the bakery's in trouble. I know! You don't have to lie about it!"

Her hands shook and shimmered as she passed JP back his phone. She could feel herself wavering in and out of sight. JP looked like he might be trying to turn invisible himself, shuffling his feet and avoiding Leo's eyes.

Poor JP. He had been dropped unexpectedly into the worst week the bakery had ever had. Leo's brain whirled through the list of terrible things, trying to make sense of it all. She and her cousin walked in silence toward the bakery, feet pounding the sidewalk.

Clomp clomp clomp. Mamá said the bakery was warded against burglars, but another heirloom was gone.

Clomp clomp clomp. As much as Leo tried to imagine a sneaky way the O'Rourkes could have made it to the bakery and back since she had left their house, it just didn't add up. They probably weren't the thieves, which meant they weren't the accomplices.

Clomp clomp clomp. Leo had wasted all this time, hurt her friends, for nothing. She was no closer to understanding Abuelo's plan.

His plan didn't make sense at all, anyway. Why would he send a thief to steal heirlooms one at a time? Having planned her share of heists, Leo was sure it was harder to break into and back out of the busy bakery twice than it was to do it just once. Unless . . .

Unless they didn't have to break into the bakery at all, because they were already welcome inside.

Leo stopped walking. After a few steps, JP turned around. "What's up?"

Leo stared at her cousin. Her Logroño cousin. JP had been approached by Abuelo Logroño and had never said anything about it. He wanted to see everything in the bakery and learn more about it. He had taken the news of the family magic pretty calmly, and he had been completely supportive of Leo's wild goose chase to spy on the O'Rourkes. He had been one of the last people to see the molcajete just before it disappeared.

He had dropped unexpectedly into the worst week the bakery had ever had.

"Leo?" JP said. "Is there a problem? Can I help?"

All the anger Leo felt, all the rage and uncertainty and fear, burned her throat, clawing to come out. She wanted to scream that she knew *exactly* how much JP wanted to help. She wanted to punch her cousin right in his sympathetic face.

But that wasn't the smart, strategic thing to do. If JP really was the accomplice, Leo needed to warn her family. And if she tried to warn them with no evidence, they wouldn't believe her. Mamá had already dismissed one of Leo's hunches, and Isabel would be disappointed that she had trusted Leo's wrong guess about the O'Rourkes. No, if Leo wanted to stop JP, she had to catch him in the act.

Besides, she might be wrong. Caroline was right that Leo shouldn't let her feelings explode and hurt the people around her. She didn't want to hurt JP the way she'd hurt her friends, or even the way she'd hurt the O'Rourkes by using magic to totally invade their privacy. She needed to be more careful. She wanted to be a bruja Mamá would be proud of, not one who followed in Abuelo Logroño's footsteps.

If she was right, then even Mamá would understand her use of magic to protect herself.

"Fine," she said out loud. "I'm fine." Her voice came out strangled, and she couldn't meet her cousin's eyes for fear he would see the suspicion burning in her mind. She was afraid she wouldn't be able to walk alongside him one more step without exploding her doubts everywhere. If JP was guilty, and if he knew she suspected him, he would be more cautious, harder to catch. She couldn't let him know, but she couldn't act like everything was normal, either.

"Okay," JP said. "Do you . . . still want to go to the bakery?"

She couldn't act like everything was normal, but maybe she could create a diversion, and catch JP just when he thought he was safe. A plan formed in her mind, a way to lure her cousin into action, if indeed he was in cahoots with Abuelo.

"This is all my fault!" Leo cried. JP flinched, Leo let go of her concentration, and by the time JP reached for her she was already invisible, running in the wrong direction down Main Street, kicking up puffs of pollen as she went.

"What do you mean, she ran away?"

Daddy's face was scrunched into wrinkles and his hair stood on end from running his fingers through it too many times. He glared at JP, who stood in the bakery doorway, mouth hanging open while Mamá, Isabel, and Marisol moved to surround him.

Leo, who had snuck in invisibly behind JP, watched the scene with a belly full of guilt.

"She said, um, that it was all her fault, and then she ran away," JP mumbled.

"Paloma?" Mamá had her phone tucked between her shoulder and her ear. "No, we didn't find it. We have another problem. It's Leo."

"Ran away where?" Daddy asked. "Why didn't you follow her?"

"Well, I . . . I'm not sure? Because . . ." JP looked at Isabel pleadingly.

"What direction?" Daddy said, his voice squeaking in frustration. "Did she go back to Caroline's house? Or toward the freeway? Was she heading toward our house? Give me something here, Juan Pablo."

JP just opened and closed his mouth.

"He doesn't know," Isabel said, coming to the younger boy's rescue. "It's not his fault. He doesn't know because—because Leo can turn invisible now."

Mamá dropped her phone. It clattered to the floor and lay there until JP picked it up and handed it back.

"Paloma? Yes, sorry. I'm going to have to call you back." Mamá hung up the phone and sagged against the counter.

"Cucaracha," Marisol whispered. "What are you doing?" That made Leo freeze on her way past the counter, but when she looked at Marisol, her sister was gazing out the front window, not actually talking to Leo.

"Is she training with . . . *him?*" Mamá asked faintly.

"No!" Isabel said while JP shook his head quickly. "Mamá, it's not like that. It's just her power. She came into it on her own. We were thinking . . . it seems like it might be her birth-order power."

"That is the last ability Leo needed," Marisol muttered under her breath.

"Okay," Mamá said slowly. "Okay." She tugged the strings of her apron and tightened her ponytail. "I'm going to scry for her."

"Elena." Daddy held up his hand. "You've done so many scrying spells this week, and they take a lot out of you, and . . . well . . ."

"They don't work very well." Marisol, as usual, had no problem being blunt. "Tía Paloma got better results from across the state."

"Hush, Marisol," Mamá snapped. "Yes, scrying

isn't my specialty, but I can make sure Leo's safe, at least."

"Tía Paloma could do that," Isabel said gently, "and she has the twins to help her conserve energy."

Mamá fumed. "Fine." She tapped her phone with quick, angry fingers.

"There's something else," JP said. "Something that happened right before we left Caroline's, I mean, Brent's, uh . . . right before Leo ran away. She sort of . . . got in a fight. With Caroline. And Brent. About . . . things."

Leo didn't want to stand there while JP tried to lie awkwardly. She moved to the kitchen instead, crawling under the swinging blue doors so she wouldn't disturb them. She had a plan to carry out.

On the top shelf of the last wooden cabinet, the bakery's magical items hid. Leo didn't know how many special heirloom artifacts her family had—she had learned about the mixing bowl and the molcajete just this month—but there was one other item she knew for sure would tempt a thief.

She needed to bait her trap.

Luckily, the kitchen was a disaster zone, turned upside down in the search for the molcajete. That made Leo's job a whole lot easier. Ms. Wood had done a whole science class on Rube Goldberg machines:

elaborate domino-effect contraptions where each part set off the next part in a complex mechanism designed to do one simple task. Leo didn't have marbles or rubber bands, but while her family argued outside about her disappearance, she carefully shifted the contents of the shelf, the position of the cabinet doors, and the mop bucket into just the right positions.

"We should go home," Mamá was saying. "Before we work ourselves into any more of a panic. Leo's smart; she might have been upset, but she wouldn't have run off to do anything dangerous."

Marisol snorted and Isabel grimaced.

"And anyway," Mamá continued, "I'm not in the mood to work anymore today. We can leave the cleanup for later. I'm not sure . . . I'm not sure if we'll open tomorrow anyway."

Leo stood just inside the kitchen doorway, wishing she could give Mamá a hug and erase the tired worry lines across her forehead.

"I'll turn off the ovens and the lights," Isabel said. She walked to the blue doors and pushed them open.

The doors knocked the mop bucket, sending it rolling across the tiled floor . . .

. . . where it knocked the second wood cabinet, jostling its ajar door more fully open . . .

. . . and into the last cabinet's door, which flapped shut with a bang, upsetting the barely balanced object hanging over the edge of the top shelf, knocking it to the floor with a slightly muffled clink.

"Everything okay in there?" Daddy called.

Leo held her breath, watching Isabel's face as she stared at the path the mop bucket had taken. Leo's plan depended on secrecy, so if Isabel figured out that someone had set all these things to fall, everything would be ruined.

"Fine!" Isabel called back. "Sorry, it's a mess in here. I'm fine."

She walked to the fallen object, small and silk wrapped, a clear crystal Mamá had once placed in Leo's palm to show her how strong her magic could be. Isabel held the crystal inside the silk, tapping her bottom lip in thought.

Come on. Leo tried to telepathically beam thoughts to her sister. *Come on, Isabel.*

"Mamá," Isabel called, "do you think we should bring the crystal with us tonight? We might not want to leave it here, considering everything that's gone missing."

Leo let out a sigh of relief as Isabel made her way back to the front of the bakery. Then she slipped out the back door and hid in the back of Daddy's truck.

Nobody would dream of connecting the crystal with Leo now, which meant that JP would have no idea that she was on to him.

And no idea that he was about to steal himself straight into a trap.

CHAPTER 18
CAUGHT!

Leo had hitched a secret ride home in Daddy's truck and raced past him when he unlocked the door, and she was innocently and visibly pouting on her bed when he rushed to check her room.

"You scared us big-time, Leonora," he scolded while he hugged her. "Don't do that again, please."

Dinner was solemn, and nobody wanted to talk unless it was to lecture Leo for being irresponsible or for not telling them about her invisibility. Leo barely touched Isabel's spaghetti, too nervous waiting for Mamá to hide the crystal.

"What's that?" she made sure to ask loudly when

Mamá slipped the silk bundle into a kitchen cupboard, followed by the family recipe book and a wooden box Leo had never seen before.

"Heirlooms," Mamá said. "We brought them for safekeeping."

In the chair next to Leo, JP seemed to be totally focused on inhaling his pasta, but Leo saw his eyes flick to the cabinet after Mamá sat back down.

Mamá wanted to "chat" with Leo, which probably meant a long lecture and then a long discussion of her new power, but Leo told her that she was worn out from a long day of magic and needed rest more than she needed to learn a lesson. Mamá agreed, but not before she confiscated Leo's herb pouch. Then Leo retreated to her room to hide until the sun set and the house settled into quiet.

That was when she got up, slipped effortlessly into the shadows, and crept into the kitchen.

Leo didn't know if JP, or whoever the thief was, was a saltasombras too, or had some way to see invisible people. So she hid in the pantry, the crack in the door giving a perfect view of the cupboard where the heirlooms slept. She sat down on a bag of dried pinto beans, stomped her feet to scare away any spiders or cucarachas or other creepy crawlies, and settled in for a long stakeout.

Only about fifteen minutes had passed, however, when she heard creaking footsteps crossing the living room.

Leo leaned forward, heart pounding as a tall figure entered the kitchen. It cut through a moonbeam coming through the window, and in that moment, Leo saw her cousin's face illuminated.

"You! I knew it!" Leo yelled as she leaped to her feet. But she forgot that JP couldn't hear her. She pulled open the pantry door, ready to confront her treacherous cousin.

But he was opening the refrigerator door, and a moment later was fumbling to stick a straw into a cardboard juice box, his hand shaking. Leo let the pantry close quietly behind her, waiting to see what he was up to.

JP sucked his juice until the straw made empty bubbling noises, then tossed it into the trash. He pulled out the leftover bowl of spaghetti, ripping off the Saran wrap and digging in without even heating up the sludgy cold mass. He didn't so much as glance at the cupboard.

"JP?" Leo stepped out of the shadows, "What are you doing?"

"Gah!" JP dropped the bowl and the fork, sending spaghetti everywhere.

Leo braced herself in case someone heard, but after a moment of silence, it was clear that everyone was still asleep.

"Marisol was right," JP grumbled once he caught his breath. "You're already so sneaky, of course your power ended up being invisibility."

Leo grabbed paper towels from the pantry. "What are you doing up in the middle of the night?" she asked as they both cleaned spaghetti off the floor.

"Low blood sugar," he answered. "What are you doing up in the middle of the night, and invisible?"

Leo hesitated. Her plan depended on JP not knowing that she suspected him.

"What?" he asked. "There's no one here to spy on, except . . ." He tilted his head and glanced toward the cupboard. "Oh, of course! A stakeout. That's smart. But why didn't you tell me you were—" His eyes widened. "Oh."

Leo shrugged guiltily.

"So you thought I was . . ." His mouth turned down. "But I don't even . . ." He shook his head. "Why does it feel like anything I say is going to make me sound guilty? Leo, I promise I didn't steal your heirlooms."

"I know." Leo sighed. A real thief likely wouldn't stop for spaghetti while pulling a heist, and JP was way too terrible a liar to have been spying for Abuelo

Logroño all along anyway. "I guess I just had to rule it out."

JP nodded slowly. "It makes sense, actually."

"You did just happen to show up at a suspicious time," Leo said.

"No . . . I mean, this must have been Abuelo Logroño's plan," JP said. "He got into your head, you know? He's got you feeling unsafe, suspecting everyone, fighting with your friends, worrying your family. I bet he thinks that if he can make you feel like you're on your own, like there's no one you can trust, you'll eventually decide you need more power to protect yourself. Then you'll turn to him."

Leo stared at her cousin as he stood and dumped his soggy paper towels into the trash. Was he right? She had thought the only way to beat Abuelo Logroño was to beat him at his own sneaky, secretive game. Mamá and Daddy hid their worries and their spells too, and wouldn't tell Leo or her sisters what they were thinking. Maybe this wasn't the way to go about things at all.

Maybe Abuelo Logroño didn't even need to sabotage the bakery to hurt Leo's family.

Leo wiped the final streak of spaghetti sauce off the floor. "I think we need to have a family meeting."

JP nodded. "And we should do it in here. We don't want Abuelo's accomplice to snatch the heirlooms while you're fixing things."

"So you spied on us, and you lied to us about spying on Belinda O'Rourke." Mamá frowned at Leo from across the table. She and Daddy had reluctantly woken up to come to Leo's family meeting, and they were still pretty groggy. Marisol and Isabel were more awake but just as confused. "And now you want to tell everyone what you learned while spying?"

Leo nodded. "I'm sorry. I thought I had to be sneaky because . . . well, because Abuelo was being sneaky, and you were being sneaky. And when I tried to tell you about my worries—"

Mamá sighed. "I guess I wasn't exactly modeling proper open communication. You girls really know how to throw my mistakes back in my face." Marisol snickered. "Okay, fine, you're right. Your father and I have been stressed, and worried. We didn't want you girls to be scared, and we thought that it was our responsibility to protect you, but I can see how that backfired. I should have told you that I've been scrying and scrubbing the house and bakery with as many positive-energy herbs as possible. Still, I haven't found any trace of whoever is stealing our things. I just don't understand it."

"I thought it was Belinda O'Rourke," Leo said. "But she and her daughter seem innocent. And then I thought it was JP, but when he had the opportunity tonight, the only thing he stole was spaghetti."

"You're always welcome to our spaghetti, JP," Isabel said softly.

"Thanks. Sorry I dumped it on the floor."

"So I don't have any answers either," Leo continued, "but it's got to be someone working with Abuelo Logroño, someone who can get through the wards. That's what Abuelo Logroño hinted at, anyway. And we know that they've been able to steal things right out from under our noses before, even while people were in the bakery."

Isabel looked at the cupboard. "So if someone's after out magical heirlooms, and the heirlooms are here, why don't we just follow through with Leo's plan? It seems like it's still our best chance to catch the thieves."

"If we haven't already tipped them off by having this obvious family meeting," Marisol muttered.

Mamá nodded slowly. "I'd prefer to know what magical plots are going on under my own roof. But I must admit, Leo's plan was a good one. And one that may still work."

Leo smiled. Before, her plan had been sitting like a knot in her stomach that she had to clutch tightly or else it would fall to pieces. Now the knot was gone, and her breathing came more easily.

"Hold on," JP said. "Does anyone hear that . . . ?"

Everyone froze. Mamá snapped her fingers, putting out the kitchen light with a burst of magic that Leo could smell in the air. Leo heard the sound, a rhythmic scuffling, just before it stopped abruptly.

In the dark, a pair of glowing eyes peeked into the kitchen doorway.

"Gatito," Mamá groaned. She snapped her fingers again, and the lights came back on. Señor Gato leaped from the floor onto the stovetop, his tail bushy as he meowed loudly. Everyone around the table laughed.

"He wants to know why everyone's up, probably," Daddy said. "And I don't blame him. It's way past my bedtime." He stood up from the table and stretched. Mamá pushed her chair back as well, making a screech that rattled the cupboards.

But one cupboard in particular rattled more than the others.

"Wait," Leo said. She held up a hand. The door of the cupboard where the heirlooms were stashed stilled, but came to rest slightly open. Almost like something was stuck in the way. . . .

Leo slipped into the shadows, and only then could she see that there, standing perfectly still on the counter with one hand reaching into the cupboard, was a small figure with bright yellow eyes and skin the greenish-orange color of dried catkin pollen. It had a round face with big eyes like a kindergartner, but its skin was as wrinkly as a grandparent's, and it wore an oversized floppy brown hat with a wide brim and pointed crown.

And it was stealing their heirlooms.

"Stop that!" Leo shouted. The creature pulled its empty hand out of the cupboard. "Mamá, the thief is here!"

She had no idea if her family could hear her, but she didn't wait to find out. She jumped on top of the counter and scrambled toward the creature, who tucked into a ball and rolled away, so fast that Leo's fingers barely grazed the tip of its hat. The thief stopped dead in the center of the kitchen, eyes flicking warily between Leo and its fallen hat on the floor in front of her.

"Leo?" Mamá asked. "What happened? Are you okay?"

The creature looked at Leo and started to shimmer. Leo turned visible too, hopping off the counter to look more closely at the upright triangular ears on top of the creature's head. "What is going on?" she asked. "What are you?"

The creature whined.

"Uh, is this normal?" JP's voice cracked, "Can somebody tell me if this is normal?"

"Not normal," Daddy answered in a whisper. Mamá patted his arm, but she also stared open-mouthed at the creature.

The thief didn't move, but another creature of the same type darted out from behind the refrigerator, faster than Señor Gato chasing a lizard, and wrapped bony fingers around Leo's toe.

"Hey!" Leo yanked her foot away and heard her toe pop like a cracked knuckle as she escaped the creature's clutches. "Cut it out! What is your problem?" She couldn't bring herself to kick something so much smaller than she was, so she reached out her free hand and snatched the red floppy hat off the second creature's head.

"Give it back give it back give it back!" She was not expecting its sudden high-pitched squeal. The creature reached for its hat, arms flailing. Señor Gato hissed from his perch on the stove.

"Okay, okay, sorry." Leo held out the hat, the surprisingly soft material slipping easily from her grasp. "Just . . . leave my toes alone. And tell me what you're doing here. Please."

The creature ruffled its wispy tufts of moss-green hair and scratched behind its cat ears before resettling its hat atop them, eyeing Leo suspiciously. Its eyes were spring green and slit pupiled, and its skin deep green and glossy like magnolia leaves. Like the first creature, it kept darting its eyes to the hat on the floor.

"Here." Leo picked up the hat and handed it back to the first creature, deciding from its gray hair and wrinkly skin that it was the older of the two. "Now, will you tell me what you're doing in my house?"

"It's not your house, hat thief," the older creature said in a gruff voice.

Leo wondered if she had fallen asleep in the pantry and was now caught in a very confusing bad dream. "*You're* the thief here," she said. "Or are you going to tell me I didn't catch you with your hand in our cupboard, trying to take our heirlooms?"

The creature wrung its hands, looking at its younger friend. They made a colorful pair, from the brown and red tips of their hats down to their earthtoned faces and their . . .

"Hey!" Leo cried. "That's my shirt!" The younger and smaller creature was wearing the neon-pink tee she had gotten at a gas station outside New Braunfels one summer, after a road-trip nacho spill ruined her normal clothes. She hadn't seen it in years. She inspected the creature's bright orange shorts and recognized them as a pair Alma and Belén had blamed each other for losing at camp, belted with a sequined scarf Isabel had gotten for a birthday and never touched.

"One of them's mine," Marisol said. She pointed at the older creature, who was wearing her purple-and-red tie-dyed shirt with plastic beads tied in a fringe on the bottom.

"You see?" Leo said. "You're a bunch of clothes thieves, and you're probably bowl thieves too, so don't call me a thief just because I grabbed your hat in . . . in self-defense of my toes!"

"Leo," JP whispered weakly. "Maybe don't make the duendes angry?"

Duendes? Leo eyed the creatures, remembering Mamá's warnings throughout her childhood about small people living hidden in the house. Leo couldn't remember what they were supposed to look like, only that she had always been afraid that if she didn't respect her bedtime or behave herself, the mysterious creatures would steal her toes.

Her toes! "You *are* duendes!" she said, curling her toes for safety. "I didn't know duendes were thieves. What do you need a mixing bowl or a molcajete for, anyway?"

JP cringed, hiding behind Marisol, who looked like she might want to hide behind him.

The creatures looked at each other, eyebrows and noses twitching. "We apologize, saltasombras," the older one said. "To you and your family. You've named us correctly as thieves. Please give us a chance to explain."

Leo looked at Mamá, who shrugged, and Isabel, who nodded. This was the reason she had set the bait in the first place. They all wanted answers. But could they trust the creatures to tell the truth?

"You're the accomplices," Leo said. "You know I'm a saltasombras because you're working with my abuelo."

The younger creature, whose face was smoother and more round cheeked, shook its head so fast it looked like it was drying off. "Not *with*," it squeaked, its big eyes filling with tears. "We don't work with magic wardens and family thieves! We apologize, but we had no choice. The shadow jumper caught our siblings, just like you caught us."

"You mean like a Pokémon," JP said, then ducked back behind Marisol when the duendes turned his way.

"But I didn't . . ." Leo frowned at the trembling point of the creature's hat. "I'm not catching you.

I mean, I caught you stealing, but I'm not going to *catch* you."

"Maybe we should start over," Daddy suggested. His voice wavered, and he took a deep breath before he continued. "Welcome to our house. I wish we could have met under better circumstances, but we promise we don't mean you any harm. We just want to know what's going on."

Leo didn't untuck her toes, but she did extend a hand toward the older creature. She'd never heard of duendes stealing fingers, so it was probably safe. "I'm Leo."

The duendes eyed her hand, still looking equal parts scared and suspicious. "You are a salta-sombras. Like the family thief."

Leo could think of lots of ways that Abuelo Logroño had done her family wrong, but she got the sense that the duendes knew something she didn't. "I don't work with him either," she said. "And I didn't know he was stealing your family. He's a bad guy. We're trying to stop him."

The old duende sighed. "This isn't the first time our family has been caught in the middle of a brujo war," it said. "We regret the harm we have done to your family, which has always been a friend to ours." It reached for Leo's hand, not shaking it, but laying its hand on top of hers before letting go.

"We have been?" Isabel asked. "Since when?"

Leo was glad she wasn't the only one who was totally confused.

"I'm afraid I'm lost as well," Mamá said. "Do you know our family?"

The duende smiled. "Will you sit with us?" it asked. Without waiting for an answer, both duendes stretched out on their stomachs on in the middle of the kitchen floor, propped up on their elbows.

"Um, I guess so. . . ." Leo copied their position, the cold tile making her shiver. She looked over her shoulder at Mamá and Daddy, who opted to sit cross-legged instead. Marisol and JP stayed standing, as far from the duendes as possible. Isabel hesitated, watching everyone before sliding down into a crouch with her legs tucked under her.

"Our extended family," the old duende began once everyone was settled, "has been called by many names. . . ."

CHAPTER 19
DUEN DE CASA

"Our extended family has been called by many names, but you know us as duendes. Etymologically, duen de casa: owner of the house. A good name, from when your human family showed us respect. We have lived alongside humans as long as they have walked these lands. Even we cannot remember a time before our family lived with yours, and our memories stretch much longer."

"Um," Leo interrupted, "are you talking about *our* family? Or just, like, humans in general?"

The duende squinted at her. "Your human family built houses on these lands," he said, "and your human family tore those houses down and built new ones, and your human family fought over which houses belonged to which of them."

Leo considered pointing out that none of that answered her question, but instead she decided to keep listening.

"Our family did not involve ourselves in those fights, out of fear, or perhaps an arrogant belief that they did not concern us. We let your family nearly destroy your family. And once they had control, their brujos turned their attention to us and tried to destroy us as well."

"Wait, who is 'they'?" Leo asked. The word "family" was starting to sound funny from being used too many times, and she was losing the thread of the story. She rubbed her eyes, wishing she could have discovered the duendes a few hours earlier.

"When humans have power, they tend to see anyone unfamiliar as a threat to that power. Your abuelo is part of a family of brujos who used power to steal, hurt, and exploit. They are enemies of my family and others. We used to be respected owners of every house, and now we are only hidden residents of a few."

Leo bit her lip. Abuelo Logroño had made himself out to be a hero, protecting humans from evil creatures. Mamá had warned her it wasn't true, but she hadn't thought about how the lie covered up a scarier truth. Abuelo was *hurting* the magical creatures.

"But your other family, the line of your mother," the duende continued, "is part of a family that did not turn its back on us, even after we turned our backs on the human family. That's why my siblings live here, and my cousins live with your aunt and in your bread house. We protect each other, even if your family forgot."

"Until Abuelo Logroño kidnapped your siblings," Leo said. "And he said that if you didn't steal from us, he'd hurt them."

The duende nodded. "He could not enter the bread house, but its guarding spells were never meant for us."

"I'm sorry," Leo said. "For my abuelo. But don't worry, we'll find a way to save your siblings, right?" She turned to Mamá and Daddy, who nodded.

The duende frowned while the younger one shook its head quickly. "Too risky," it said. "We want our siblings back safely. We don't want to fight a magic warden."

"We'll be careful," Leo said. "We can come up with a plan."

"I might have one, actually," Isabel said, tugging the end of her ponytail thoughtfully. "You won't have to fight. We would just need you to help set the trap."

"Trap?" the duende asked.

"We'll discuss the plan," Mamá said, putting her hand on Isabel's shoulder as Isabel rose. "If you can convince him to meet with you, then we can handle the rest."

"We have to meet with him," the young duende said. "Tomorrow. To trade one stolen crystal for one stolen sibling. Are you sure you can help?"

"Don't worry," Leo said. "This is kind of what we do."

The old duende tilted its head all the way sideways and peered at Leo. "You are a strange member of the human family."

Marisol snorted. "Tell me about it."

"And you promise none of my family will be hurt?" The duende looked at each human in turn.

"I promise," Leo said. "We'll fix this."

From the top of the stove, Señor Gato meowed.

"I understand your concern, distant cousin," the old duende said. "But I know you wouldn't have adopted them if they were not a special human family."

Señor Gato only replied with a flick of his tail.

* * *

The family meeting lasted late into the night. After moving everyone back to the kitchen table instead of the floor, Mamá made tea for them all except the duendes, who asked for hot chicken broth instead.

"Is it always like this at your house?" JP whispered to Leo while Mamá questioned the duendes on the spells Abuelo Logroño had used to capture their siblings.

Leo thought of the magical emergencies they'd had before. "Sometimes. But definitely more than usual this week. That's part of the reason I suspected that you were behind it."

JP nodded. "Well, I'm glad I'm not. Aunt Elena is scary when she gets down to business. I would hate to be on her bad side."

"You were right, you know; I did let Abuelo Logroño get into my head," she said sheepishly. "And it turns out that all my hunches were completely one hundred percent dead wrong."

"Well, your problem was not thinking to check for little cat goblin borrowers who've been living in your house since time immemorial." JP shrugged. "Rookie mistake."

Leo laughed.

"But I'm not the only one you should be telling this

to," JP continued. He reached into the pocket of his plaid pajama pants and held his phone out to her, under the table so Mamá and Daddy wouldn't see.

Leo took the phone, stomach flipping over itself. "Thanks." She tucked the phone into her own pocket and excused herself to go to the bathroom.

Hi, it's Leo.

She texted Caroline first to build up her courage. She wanted to call to hear her friend's voice, but it was so late it was early, and waking her friend from the middle of sleep didn't seem like a great way to start an apology.

I'm sorry I was a jerk yesterday, Leo typed. **I'm sorry I didn't trust you. You were right anyway, but even if I was right, I was being the worst. And maybe a little jealous. So I hope we're still friends. Except I'll try to be a better one.**

She thought for a moment, then typed some more.

Oh, also there are duendes living in my house and we're plotting to defeat my abuelo. I'm not asking for help this time, but thanks for always helping me with plans. Talk to you later, I hope. Good morning.

She pulled up a new message to Brent next, but guilt made it hard to know where to start. Eventually she found a DragonBlood gif, where the main character knelt in front of the injured queen of dragons. *I am not worthy to be called your friend,* the caption read. Leo hit send.

I'm sorry for being mean, she typed. **I'll bake you anything you want after we defeat my grandpa if you forgive me. This is Leo, by the way.**

She felt a twinge of relief as she sent the messages, then hurried back to the kitchen, hoping that the new plot would keep her mind off JP's phone.

"The problem is that Álvaro has so many tricks up his sleeve," Mamá was saying. "With the help of your family"—she nodded at the duendes—"we know what we're up against, and we will have the element of surprise, but that only buys us one shot. Saving the duende hostages is our first priority, but if we use our surprise attack to release them and help them escape, that leaves us to duel Álvaro head-on, and I'm afraid our magic isn't up to the task."

"I mean, I offered to just whack him with a frying pan," Marisol muttered. "It feels like you're not open to my suggestions at all."

"What if our first move, before we even release the duendes, was to block his magic?" Isabel asked. "There are wards for that; I saw them in Tía Paloma's book when we were renewing the physical wards around the house."

"Speed is still the issue," Mamá said. "Anything we could work quickly would be limited to shutting down one of his abilities. We could stop him from turning invisible, but it wouldn't affect his illusion spells. Or we could cut off his illusions, but he would still be able to harm the hostages with offensive spells. A more complicated ward would require so many steps, I can't think how we'd be able to surprise him with it."

"A recipe?" Isabel asked. "We do lots of complicated spells in recipes, and they act instantaneously."

"Yeah, but I somehow doubt this criminal mastermind is going to willingly eat a snack offered by a bruja cocinera," Marisol pointed out.

While her sisters bounced ideas like rubber balls across the table, Leo poured tea and broth refills.

"This is why it makes more sense to study broadly." Isabel sighed. "There's so much more magic than just what's passed down in our recipe book. I mean, even if you worked more on your scrying, Mamá—"

"My scrying is fine." Mamá frowned. "It's not our aptitude."

"But that doesn't mean you should ignore it," Isabel said. "Don't you want to learn more? There are so many types of magic, and we barely even touch them."

"Where is this coming from?" Mamá asked, her face turning stormy.

"It's coming from the fact that we've got our backs against the wall right now," Isabel said. "And if we spent a little more time learning new techniques instead of burying our heads in old traditions, we wouldn't be!"

"I think we're getting a little bit off track here." Daddy spread his hands and spoke soothingly. "Isabel, I know you're frustrated about the situation, but that's no reason to—"

Mamá cut him off with a hand on his. "Isabel," she said, "it seems like something is bothering you."

"I don't want to go to school in San Antonio!" Isabel said.

Mamá and Daddy gaped. The duendes absorbed themselves with straightening the brims of their hats. Marisol dropped her head into her hands. "Now?" she whispered quietly. "We're doing this now?"

"I got accepted in New Orleans," Isabel said, "and I want to go. There are dozens of folks from the Southwest Regional Brujería and Spellcraft Association there, and I could learn so much. There's even tuition help and class credit for brujería and spellcraft independent study—it's sort of secret, but I've talked to the program head about it."

From the way the words tumbled out of Isabel's mouth, Leo could tell her sister had planned this speech down to every last argument. But how could she want to leave Texas for four whole years? Instead of being a few hours away, she would be separated by a whole day of driving. Leo couldn't believe Isabel had kept this secret from her, and from everyone.

"Is this the best moment?" Marisol hissed again in the stunned silence. Isabel shrugged, breathing like she had just worked through a midmorning rush.

So Marisol had known already. Mamá's mouth was still hanging open and her eyes were wide. She was probably more hurt and surprised than Leo.

"I just don't want to be stuck running the bakery forever," Isabel said. "There's a lot more to learn outside of Rose Hill."

Daddy cleared his throat and rubbed his eyes. "Sorry about this," he said to the guests at the table. The two duendes, perched atop booster seats made of books and overturned pots, tilted their heads at him and Isabel.

"No need to apologize," the older duende said. "We

are happy to have the help of a family that values the well-being of each of its members."

"Of course we do," Mamá said, finally finding her voice. "Isabel, of course we'll support you, whatever you want to do. I'm sorry that I assumed . . . well, let's talk more after all this."

Isabel nodded, and the whole family returned to discussing the best way to attack Abuelo Logroño. But Leo wasn't ready to move on yet. Isabel didn't want to run the bakery when she grew up? Her whole life, Leo had imagined a future where she helped Isabel the way Tía Paloma helpd Mamá: working together to keep Amor y Azúcar thriving, cooking up delicious breads and pastries and special magical spells alike.

But, when Leo thought about it, Isabel had always been more interested in perfecting her spells than her kneading. She liked weaving complex recipes for the special orders the bakery received, but she hated running the cash register, part of the reason Marisol had always done more sales and inventory than magic. Leo imagined Isabel in New Orleans, studying with spell casters and other brujas, learning all types of magic. It was an unfamiliar scene, but it made sense.

She just didn't know what it meant for the bakery.

". . . Nightshades work as antidotes to aconite," Mamá was saying. "So with the right intention, we could use potatoes or tomatoes to weaken his invisibility. Even goji berries—I think Paloma got some dried ones a few weeks ago because she wanted to experiment with substituting them. . . ."

"I saw all those binding spells when we were building the portal in January," Isabel said. "I'm sure I could improvise one using some combination of sugar and salt. . . ."

"Maybe he wouldn't notice if we just happened to have a circle of candles around the room?" Marisol suggested, not looking very hopeful.

Leo always felt out of her depth in conversations like this. There were so many herbs and ingredients, and in spite of memorizing plenty of them during her lessons with Tía Paloma, Leo couldn't call them to the top of her head at a moment's notice the way Mamá and Isabel could. The ideas and suggestions filled her head too fast and congealed into mush too thick to let her think of anything herself. Her brain was like capirotada, sticky and bursting with a million ingredients. Ingredients like almonds to cancel negative energy . . .

. . . sweet cinnamon syrup and salty cheese and dried berries . . .

. . . leftover bread, like the day-old bolillos that carried Amor y Azúcar's power inside their slightly dried-out crusts.

"Mamá," she said, "I think I have an idea."

CHAPTER 20
CAPIRO-TA-DA!

By midmorning, the bakery was open, and the plan was underway. While Mamá and Isabel filled the shelves with a normal day's worth of baked goods, Leo ripped bolillos into chunks and soaked them with syrup made of brown sugar and cinnamon. She then mixed in almonds soaked in rainwater for purification, dried goji berries for their ability to reveal what was once hidden, and chunks of salted cheese to carry the power of Isabel's binding spell. On the counter in front of her loomed a tall pile of cake pans and casserole dishes, everything that could be spared in the bakery plus what they had brought from home.

"Are you sure that I should be the one to make it?" Leo had asked when Mamá assigned her to the task. She had expected to be working the register, or maybe pumping out a steady supply of bolillos.

"It was your idea," Mamá said. "And for this to have the best chance of working, you'll be the one to initiate everything. So if you feel up to it, I'd like you to do the preparation. Is that okay, 'jita?"

Leo had almost glowed with pride. Mamá wasn't giving her the easiest job, or the one no one else wanted. She trusted Leo with real magic. Leo balled her fists and smiled. All week she'd wanted to show Abuelo Logroño how wrong he was about her family and their powers. This was her chance to do it.

Now sweat covered her brow as she filled pan after pan and slotted each into the oven, concentrating on pouring her magic into every nook, cranny, and crunchy corner of the capirotada. And every time a warm pan left the oven, Leo sliced it into bite-sized squishy squares and plopped it onto the front counter in front of Daddy, right next to a Marisol-designed sign that read *FREE SAMPLES!*

JP had put himself on dirty-dish duty, weaving between bakers to clear counters at lightning speed. "This is kind of fun," he told Leo as he passed with an armful of dirty spoons and spatulas. "Have you ever played one of those apps where you run a busy kitchen? It's just like that!"

The duendes had disappeared into the dark corners of the bakery. Leo thought it would have been nice of them to at least offer to help prepare for the plan. She was pretty sure she could trust them to complete their part of the trap, but their disappearance didn't exactly inspire confidence.

Plus, if she was totally honest, she had expected them to be a little more grateful for the help. But then, they had said that they were distant cousins of cats.

Leo worked steadily until lunchtime. She was washing her hands and swallowing her last bite of torta, ready to jump back onto the capirotada production line, when the front bell rang and two familiar voices called her name.

Leo dropped her day-old bread bits and rushed to greet Caroline and Brent. Once she faced them, though, her stomach flip-flopped and her own nasty voice echoed in her ears with all the mean things she had said yesterday.

"Um, hi," she said. "Did you get my texts?"

Caroline nodded and opened her mouth, but Brent pushed past her to brandish a piece of paper in Leo's face.

"We figured it out! You were right, sort of. There was something fishy going on. But we were right too—look!"

Leo took the paper he was waving, smoothing out the winkles to reveal a faded but familiar color scheme.

"The Honeybees logo," she said. "You already showed me this."

"Yes, but look carefully." Brent jabbed at the center of the paper, nearly poking a hole straight through it. "Read the fine print."

Leo squinted at the green-and-yellow lettering, which was even harder to read on an old printout. "'Honeybees Café,'" she said, just like the logo on the website, and underneath, "'Coffee, tea, and . . . artisanal honey'? What about baked goods?"

"Exactly!" Brent pointed at Leo, which was more confusing than helpful.

"So . . . they changed it? When? Why?"

"That's what we wanted to know," Caroline said. "So we went back to see Becky this morning."

If Leo still felt a tiny twinge of jealousy that her friends had gone to hang out with the new girl again, it was mostly eclipsed by the warm relief that her friends still cared enough to investigate her problems and to talk to her about them.

"With a little bit of digging," Caroline continued, "we found out that Mrs. O'Rourke always wanted to open a teahouse, but that she never thought to sell baked goods until a couple of months ago. Becky said her mom talked to a consultant, some friend of a friend, but she couldn't remember anything about him or which friend of hers he knew. Sounds fishy, right?"

Leo nodded slowly.

"So you think our grandpa planted the idea in Mrs. O'Rourke's head months ago so that she might start a rival bakery here in Rose Hill?" JP had entered the front of the bakery, and he leaned over Leo's shoulder to see the original logo better. "How did he know to do that?"

"He might have been planning this for a while," Leo said. "Maybe he found out about my magic when I started using it in January. Maybe he decided he wanted to train me then, but he knew I might not want to, or that Mamá might not let me. Plus he needed some time to capture and blackmail the duendes."

"The what?" Brent asked.

She and JP filled in their friends as quickly as possible, even though Caroline kept interrupting them to ask about different duende stories and

legends and Brent kept interrupting to make strangled noises of confusion.

"Isn't it risky to work with them?" Caroline
asked. "I mean, they've already spied on you and
stolen things for your abuelo."

Leo thought about the duendes and their strange
mannerisms. "I believe they hate him, but they're
also afraid of him. I guess that's why they won't
fight. But I think they want us to win. I trust them."

"And you're sure your recipe will work on your
grandpa?" Brent asked. "If I were him, I definitely
wouldn't touch any of your baked goods."

Leo smiled. That was the part of the plan she
liked best of all. "We've got it covered."

"Okay." Caroline smiled. "So how can we help?"

She stiffened in surprise when Leo threw one arm
around her and the other around Brent, but then
she put her own arms out to complete the group hug.

"What's this for?" Brent asked.

"I don't know," Leo said. They all let go. "Thanks
for not being mad at me."

"I still am, a little," Brent said. "I'm just putting
it aside right now because your family might lose
their bakery and their magic if this goes wrong.
So . . . what are you thinking?"

Leo really didn't deserve her friends, but she was

happy she had them. "I think it would be good to see what happens to Mrs. O'Rourke when we try to break my grandpa's spells," she said. "If he used magic to change her mind about Honeybees, then she might snap out of it. But I'm not sure how it works, and it would be nice to have y'all there to keep an eye on things. Think you could invite yourselves over to Becky's this evening?"

"That won't be a problem," Caroline said. "Especially if we bring over a board game."

"I bet I'm going to be way better at Catan now," Brent said. "I'm getting a crash course in plotting."

"Oh, and one last thing," Leo said. "Can you both eat some capirotada?"

Her friends, unsurprisingly, were happy to help with that part.

After a long day of business and free samples, Mamá closed the bakery half an hour early, with everyone too nervous to wait on any last-minute customers. Leo mopped with urgency instead of hanging around letting Isabel take care of it, and it seemed like everyone else had the same energy, because the long list of closing chores shrank like a pat of butter in a hot pan. All too soon Mamá flicked off the lights, leaving the kitchen dim with the evening sun starting to set through the windows.

The whole family loaded into Mamá's minivan, carrying boxes and cooking supplies out and running back into the kitchen for one last load before finally pulling away, creating enough chaos that anybody spying on the bakery would never notice that Leo was left inside.

The first part of the plan was complete.

Leo tiptoed back through the unlocked back door. Now that she was wrapped in shadows herself, she could see the duendes from last night in the center of the kitchen, whispering to each other. They were joined by another family member, in a black hat, whose skin was pale green with a pink-and-yellow pattern of a flower blooming around each eye,

"Is everything set up on your end?" Leo asked. "You sent a message with the meeting time?"

The old duende dipped its head in a slow nod. "Your abuelo will be here as soon as we give the signal that all is clear," it said. "Your kitchen area is the heart of your family's magic and is quite well warded against intruders like your grandfather, but we can circumvent the spells guarding the front of the store, so he will meet us out there." The duende nodded at the front of the bakery. "That's where we will deliver the object as planned."

The second duende touched the tip of the third duende's black hat. "Our cousin will communicate with your family at your aunt's house when the time is right. What happens next will be up to you."

Leo took a deep breath. She was almost past her fear that her spell would simply fail to work—her confidence in her magical ability was growing fast, and she knew the feel of a recipe that hummed with magic by now. But even with all her family's help and preparation, there was so much that could go wrong. Abuelo Logroño had powerful magic, magic that threatened helpless magical creatures and crept into the minds of innocent honey enthusiasts. Even Mamá had been afraid to face him directly.

There was no time to worry about it, though. The third duende was already nodding deeply to its cousins, and then it tugged sharply on the long tip of its hat and disappeared with a *pop*. The two duendes looked at Leo expectantly.

She nodded. "Send the signal."

The young duende opened its mouth and let out a hair-raising screech. It started at a pitch that made Leo's teeth hurt and then quickly rose until it was so high that she could no longer hear it, like a dog whistle. It was a neat trick—Leo wished Señor Gato could make his yowling too high for the human ear.

After about thirty seconds, the duende closed its

jaws. "He will come," it said. "Prepare yourself."

Leo pulled a stool next to the swinging kitchen doors and perched so she could peek through the crack between the hinges, legs tucked up so her feet wouldn't show. With only a little bit of struggling, she managed to go invisible too, just for good measure.

The front door lock clicked smoothly, which never happened when Mamá used the old scratched-up key that took several moments of wiggling and coaxing most mornings. Leo had never thought about using magic to unlock a door. Maybe this was the sort of thing Isabel meant when she said she wanted to learn skills beyond the family traditions.

But then again, Leo had never thought of using magic to kidnap and manipulate people either.

The tolling of the front-door bell sounded soft and ghostly in the dark, and Leo leaned forward to see Abuelo Logroño, his gray hair slicked back and shiny, stride into the bakery. He wasn't even bothering to walk in the shadows, though his flip-flops were, for the moment, invisible under his perfectly arranged robes. He was holding a small metal cage, like a pet carrier, but the bars glowed with harsh white light. Curled up inside was a baby duende, its chubby wrinkled skin brown like potting soil with sandy sprinkled freckles, one triangular ear poking out of its pointy knit cap.

Leo put a hand over her mouth and bit down on the web of skin between her thumb and forefinger. Her invisibility popped like a bubble, and tears blurred her view. Once she recovered from the shock, she sank back into sadness and invisibility. She had known Abuelo was a monster, but that didn't make it any easier to see him with a child in a cage.

"Well?" Abuelo Logroño spoke. "I don't have much time. Do you have it?"

The old duende stepped forward in the dark. It held out the silk-wrapped bundle to Abuelo Logroño.

Leo held her breath. Silence pushed against the walls of the bakery and squeezed her chest tight.

"Funny, isn't it?" Abuelo Logroño's voice sounded smug as he set the cage on the floor behind him. "A week ago you assured me it was impossible to rob these homespun brujas, that their wards were just too powerful. And yet with just one day of distraction—and the right motivation, of course— you dismantled those wards so completely that I can walk through the front door. You bichos continue to be a disgrace to the power you could yield. You prefer to be weak."

Leo chewed a cuticle. Just because the duendes

had the power to rob people and chose not to didn't make them weak.

"Your time is short," the old duende reminded the brujo calmly. Leo wished it had said something more rebellious. But she saw a tension in the duende's shoulders and a stillness it its stance that reminded her of Señor Gato about to pounce.

"Hmph." Abuelo Logroño stepped forward, reaching for the silk-covered lump, large in the duende's palm but small in Abuelo's grasp.

"You're certain this is the artifact?" he asked. "It feels soft. . . ."

With a few tugs he unfolded the silk wrapper to reveal the contents: a squishy, lumpy scoop of Leo's capirotada.

Almost half a year ago, Leo had sat in the back of the busy bakery and begged to try a spell on her own, her first taste of magic. It was a simple spell, endlessly adaptable, the sort of thing Isabel would add to the family recipe book because Isabel had always been most interested in breaking down and understanding the details of magic, all its rules and possibilities. It was the same spell Leo had used to dramatically reveal her power to Caroline, before her friend knew anything about her own magic. It was the spell that had first connected Leo to her power, and she reached for that connection now, focusing on the smell, taste, and feel of magic and pouring it straight into the food in her abuelo's open hand.

The capirotada burst like cascarones hitting the sidewalk, like a piñata spilling its sweets, like backyard fireworks. Bits flew in every direction, splattering Abuelo Logroño's black robes, sticking in his hair, and coating his face.

The duendes shot past the stunned brujo, so fast Leo barely saw them surround the cage before they disappeared with a tug of their hats and a double popping noise, leaving the metal cage broken and empty behind them. Just moments later, the front door opened wide as Mamá walked in, followed by Isabel and Marisol, Daddy and JP, Tía Paloma, and two dragon hunters straight out of the DragonBlood movie.

Alma and Belén had left the con early to make it back in time, but they hadn't given up their cosplay yet.

Leo jumped off the stool and shook off her shadows, joining the rest of her family as they formed a circle around Abuelo Logroño, who was still stunned by the explosion and frozen by the capirotada's spell. His arms trembled, hovering in an attempt to shield his face, unable to move.

"Álvaro," Mamá said curtly. "You've sunk to a new low since last I saw you."

"One flashy trick isn't going to stop me." Abuelo Logroño strained to respond. "And I have other duendes hidden away who might come to harm if anything happens to me."

No snappy comeback or annoying small talk, Leo noted. He had turned immediately to threats. He must be rattled.

"The duendes are taking care of their siblings," Daddy said. "They're not much for dueling, but they're quite good at reconnaissance, as I'm sure you know. They know exactly where you're keeping your prisoners, and they've been waiting for an opportunity to free them all."

The confidence in the old brujo's eyes soured. He tried to turn his head to look at Daddy but couldn't manage. "Well, I guess it's over then," he said. "Pat yourselves on the back and eat a cookie. You've won."

"Not so fast." Alma brandished her cardboard broadsword.

"We're not done with you yet," Belén added.

"You look ridiculous," Abuelo Logroño muttered, which was pretty unfair coming from a petrified old man in wizard robes and flip-flops.

"A traditional ward wasn't enough to keep you

away," Tía Paloma said. "But our family is nothing if not creative. We decided to learn some new tricks from you: instead of renewing protections on our buildings, we're going straight for the source of the problem."

"A restriction spell?" Abuelo Logroño asked. "You don't know how."

"We *didn't*," Mamá corrected him. "It turns out that your victims have seen it performed often enough to know the spell by heart. You never even thought about the danger of teaching the duendes how to sever someone's magic, did you?"

"Not one of you has the power for something like that," Abuelo Logroño hissed.

Tía Paloma shook her head. "You still don't get it. It will never be just one of us." She nodded to Isabel, who stood closest to the front counter. Marisol helped the oldest Logroño sister collect the pans and pie tins of capirotada that lined the counter, passing them down the circle until everyone held one. Leo inhaled the sweet spice scent and gripped the edges of her tin tightly.

"I hear you've been telling my daughter lies," Mamá said. "Saying that our magic lives in this building, this business. You misunderstand everything our antepasadas created." She turned her head so that she was looking straight at Leo. "Yes, this kitchen holds great power, like the mixing bowl and the molcajete and the crystal. But the bakery was only a very large heirloom, not an anchor. It was never the source of our power."

Pride and relief hummed in Leo's chest at Mamá's words. Isabel, standing next to Leo but with her hands full of capirotada, bumped her shoulder. "I didn't know either," she whispered, "until I told Mamá and Tía Paloma what you told me about the bakery, just before we came here."

"With no anchor, power cannot be channeled or passed with any meaningful consistency," Abuelo Logroño spat. "If I was mistaken, it's because I gave your operation too much credit. You're as disorganized as the duendes, letting your power grow and wither as it will, failing to properly cultivate it. And that's why I'm stronger than you." He moved suddenly, wiping crumbs off his face and chest and raising both hands as he shimmered out of sight.

"Now!" Mamá shouted. Leo dropped her pie tin to the floor and clasped hands with Alma on her right and Isabel on her left. She closed her eyes and held tight as a loud series of crashes rang in her ears.

When she opened her eyes, Abuelo Logroño was

back in the center of the circle, his hair ruffled and his face furious.

"This is hardly a binding circle." He spoke softly, and it sounded even more threatening than a shout. "Cake on the floor? Holding hands like schoolchildren? You even enlisted weak links with no power to help you." He turned and ran toward the front door, hitting the spot where Daddy and JP clasped hands. There was another crash, and Abuelo Logroño stumbled back from the edge of the circle.

"Isabel." Mamá nodded. Isabel dropped Leo's hand and began to walk clockwise around the circle.

"Your powers will fail you when you try to do harm," she said.

Leo joined her voice with everyone in the circle, repeating after Isabel once loudly, then a second time whispered. When Isabel had circled seven times, she turned and began again in the opposite direction.

"Your lies will unravel. Your cages will crumble. What you hide will be revealed."

Abuelo Logroño tried to rush the empty space Isabel had left in the circle, but he crashed into it, just the same as before.

Isabel finished her seventh orbit and rejoined the circle. She nodded one, twice, three times.

"Álvaro Logroño." The whole circle chanted in unison.

"Álvaro Logroño." A white mist began to rise from the pie tins at their feet, creating a half sphere like an upside-down bowl as it rose, staying inside the boundaries of their clasped hands.

"Álvaro Logroño." The third chant ended, and along with the rest of her family, Leo raised her foot and stomped down hard on the capirotada on the floor in front of her.

There were nine squelching thumps, and the mist rushed like water down a drain, swirling inward to sink into Abuelo Logroño's skin. By the time Leo pulled her shoe out of the sticky mess, there was no sign of the mist at all.

Abuelo Logroño sprawled on the floor, breathing heavily, one flip-flop lost and his bare foot sticking out of his robe. He pointed a hand at Mamá, face screwed up with rage, but nothing happened. Leo breathed a sigh of relief.

"You're all naive." Abuelo Logroño coughed as he spoke. "This was all flash and no substance. Your spell won't last."

"Maybe not forever," Tía Paloma said. "But then again, it might. It has over a hundred wills linked to it. Everyone who took our samples today, all our friends and family, helping to hold up the spell. This whole town is a web, and I feel confident you'll be tangled for a good long while."

Abuelo Logroño's face went slack, his mouth hanging open. He coughed several more times, but he couldn't seem to speak.

"That part," Mamá said, smiling, "was Leo's idea. You were right, you know. She's going to be a great bruja. In fact, she already is."

"And I'm going to be a great baker too," Leo added, heart swelling as she smiled at Mamá. "And part of the greatest family ever. Mine."

Daddy and JP dropped their hands, leaving the path to the front door clear.

"Go home, Álvaro," Daddy said. "You're not welcome here."

"Get a new hobby," JP suggested. "It's the twenty-first century. You can watch Netflix instead of oppressing people."

Abuelo Logroño staggered to his feet. There was something pitiful in his posture, but Leo didn't feel sorry for him. For the first time since her first dreamlike encounter with her abuelo, she felt calm and clearheaded. She left the circle to stand in front of him.

"I am going to be a saltasombras," she said, "and

I don't need your training to do it. I won't be anything like you. I'll make my own way."

Abuelo Logroño turned his face away. He walked slowly, one flip-flop in his hand, across the tiles. The front-door bell rang as he left, and they all watched him through the window, completely visible in the moonlight, growing smaller as he continued down the street.

CHAPTER 21
THE CLEANUP

Leo swirled the mop over the last sticky patch of the bakery floor, watching syrup melt into the dingy warm water. Dishes clanged behind the blue doors, and JP perched on the counter with Alma and Belén, all of them keeping their feet out of the way as they chatted excitedly about the spell, the convention, and DragonBlood.

"I'll get that." Daddy walked back into the front of the bakery and took the mop from Leo's hands. "I was just taking a call from our landlord. Turns out he made a calculation error with our rent increase. No idea how it happened." He winked. "But it's all straightened out now."

Leo joined her sisters and cousin on the counter, kicking her feet and smiling. Abuelo Logroño had cast spells on people to trick then into hurting the bakery, and now those spells were failing, the illusions cleared away like a mopped-up mess. "Can you text Caroline?" she asked JP. "I want to hear if the O'Rourkes came to their senses too."

"I don't think I have to." JP nodded at the window. Two familiar blond figures were walking toward the bakery.

Leo slid off the counter, almost slipping on the tiles below in her excitement. She threw open the front door to let Caroline and Brent in, ignoring Daddy as he cautioned them about the wet floor.

"Sorry, Mr. Logroño," Caroline said, watching her feet leave tracks as Leo pulled her inside.

"I'll forgive you if you have more good news," Daddy said. Mamá, Tía Paloma, Isabel, and Marisol entered the front of the bakery, wiping soapy hands on their aprons, all looking hopefully at Caroline and Brent. "Leo tells us you were checking in on things with Honeybees?"

Caroline twirled her ring around her finger. "We were just at the O'Rourkes' house, yeah." She sighed. "We could definitely tell when your abuelo's spell was broken. We were talking about Honeybees with Becky and her mom, and then suddenly . . .

well, I guess your abuelo used magic to make Becky agree to move here? Because the moment the spell broke, she started crying, upset with her mom for dragging her all the way to Texas."

"Oh no!" Leo hadn't imagined there could be any negative consequences to getting rid of mind-controlling illusions.

"Don't worry," Isabel said. "It's good that the spell was broken—using magic to control emotions over long periods of time can have horrible effects."

Marisol coughed a word that sounded rude.

Isabel scowled. "Over long periods of time," she repeated. "I never use my power to— Anyway, my point is that even if Becky is upset, it's best that her real emotions have been released."

"But what about Belinda?" Mamá asked.

"We had a plan," Caroline said, a little too quickly. "As soon as we suspected that the spell was lifted, we put the old Honeybees logo where they would find it."

"Becky saw it," Brent continued, "and she told her mom she wished they were sticking to the original plan, and Mrs. O'Rourke acted confused for a minute because they couldn't remember where the idea for starting a bakery came from anyway."

"That's great!" Leo said.

"Not exactly," said Caroline, averting her eyes. "Mrs. O'Rourke . . . she didn't want to go back to the honey plan. She said that wherever the idea for the bakery came from, it made sense. She said it was about time Rose Hill got an 'update.' That her modern twist on everyone's favorite baked goods would make for a thriving business."

Leo exhaled slowly, disappointment filling her chest in place of air. After a long pause, Daddy went back to mopping furiously.

"She's wrong, though," JP said. "Isn't she?"

Mamá straightened her apron. "In the interest of modeling more honesty for you kids," she said, "I'm going to say that we're concerned. Belinda is a good businesswoman."

"Our rent staying where it is will help," Daddy said. "But I think we have to consider the possibility that Amor y Azúcar is in for a tough fight."

"We should sic a dragon on her," Alma grumbled.

"Or some ghosts," Belén said. "I bet nobody wants to go to a haunted bakery." She hesitated. "Wait, no, that sounds super cool actually. Should we start advertising ourselves as a haunted bakery?"

"What if you put a spell on Mrs. O'Rourke?" Brent asked.

"We didn't stop a manipulative old brujo just to

start playing his same games," Tía Paloma said. "Hexing people is not what we do."

Mamá nodded. "I'd rather lose the bakery than teach my girls to step on other people as a way to get what they want."

Leo walked to Mamá's side and hugged her. "You're the best teacher," she whispered.

"So that's it?" Brent asked. "You're not going to do anything? Mrs. O'Rourke just gets to steal your menu and threaten your business because she wants to? That's not fair. You might not want to use your magic, but I'm going to . . . I don't know, start a protest or something. We can stand outside the Honeybees building and carry signs and shout things at people walking in."

"That's very sweet," Daddy said. "But I'm afraid that might backfire for us."

"Well, we should do *something*," Brent said.

Leo felt so much fondness for her friends and family, the way they solved one another's problems and cared about each other. But her mood was soured by the heavy realization that Abuelo Logroño's plot might still be able to hurt them, even though his spells had been defeated.

"I'd like to circle back to the ghost idea," Belén said. "A haunted bakery could be a good tourist attraction to make up for lost business."

"There shouldn't be any lost business," JP argued. "I'm with Brent; we should find a way to stop them."

"Humans." The soft voice startled them all, and Daddy dropped the mop, almost hitting the poor old duende who had snuck up on them. "Please, find peace, humans."

Caroline and Brent recovered slowest, gasping and ogling the creature until JP tugged them behind the counter by their elbows.

"Hello," Leo said. "How did it go? Did you save all your siblings?"

"Thanks to your family, yes," The old duende dipped its head. "Now we have nothing to fear from the brujo who tormented our family in this town and many others. We have peace, and now we would like to bring peace to you."

"That's nice of you," Mamá said, "but don't worry. We're happy to know that you're safe, and that you're here. My oldest daughter is excited to research more about our shared history."

The duende nodded again. "We have made a habit of retreating, to avoid the dangers of the human family, especially brujos who wanted us to side with them against others. We do not like fights. But we recognize that even inaction can cause harm, as it has done now. We knew of the saltasombras's plot long before you did. We should have warned you.

If he had been stopped earlier, he would not have planted a harmful idea so deeply in the mind of your rival relative."

Mamá shrugged. "I do hope next time you'll give us a heads-up! But it isn't your fault."

"Still, we wish to remedy the harm we have caused," the duende said.

"I'm sure one day you'll have a chance to," Mamá said. "Thank you."

The duende bowed and tugged the end of its hat, making Caroline shriek as it disappeared.

"Funny little guy, isn't he?" Daddy said.

"What makes you think she's a boy?" Alma asked. "She looked like an abuela to me."

"Cats are hard to gender," Caroline whispered, eyes still wide.

"Maybe they don't think that stuff matters very much," JP said. "They're supposed to be wise, right?"

"Hey!" Isabel called from the kitchen doorway. "The dishes are gone!"

Leo rushed to her sister's side, heart pounding. They couldn't be facing another thief, could they? But she laughed when she saw what Isabel meant.

The pile of dirty capirotada pans was sparkling clean, the sink rinsed, and even the dishrags dry and folded on the counter.

"I knew I liked those little goblins." Marisol smiled. "Do you think they'll do this every day from now on?"

"Hey, no fair, that was my new job," JP said. "What am I going to do to be helpful now?"

Daddy patted his head. "I bet we can find you some baking work," he offered. "Right, Elena?"

Mamá smiled. "Only if you want to, JP. But for tonight, let's go home and take a break."

"Yeah," Alma said. "We beat the bad guy today."

Leo wished it felt like more of a triumph.

The next two days of break passed with board games, baking—and a quiet worry that reminded Leo of hurricane season. It was nice to have the twins back in town, but Mamá had to limit them and Caroline to no more than two candles around the cash register after their many prosperity spells almost set a stack of receipts on fire. Tricia and Mai came back from their vacations, and Caroline organized a special mini snack club meeting so that JP and Becky could join in. Leo realized her friends were right about Becky—she was fun to hang out with. Especially now that she was almost as upset about her mom's business as Leo was.

It was the day before Easter—which was also

the day before JP's mom came back into town—and when Leo flipped the bakery sign from *CLOSED* to *OPEN* at seven a.m., she found Belinda O'Rourke sitting on the steps. Mrs. O'Rourke wore stretchy pants and a faded T-shirt, and her hair hung limp over her dark, tired eyes.

"Is Elena here?" she asked.

Leo nodded, too shocked to speak.

Mrs. O'Rourke followed her through the blue doors, past Isabel teaching Marisol her concha assembly-line trick, past Alma and Belén using the returned mixing bowl for bolillo production, and past Leo's early-morning baking experiment, a batch of special-occasion scones iced with pastel frosting that she wanted to serve for Easter breakfast.

Leo wasn't the only one with her ear pressed to the office door as Mamá sat down with Mrs. O'Rourke, but she was the only one who could vanish when Mamá stuck her head out and shooed away JP and Leo's sisters.

"Sorry about them," Mamá said, closing the door. Leo leaned against it to hear the muffled answer.

"My daughter is the same way. She's the one who sent me here. Sometimes I think she believes she's the one taking care of me."

"I'm surprised to see you here," Mamá said.

"Yes, well. I moved back a few weeks ago."

"That's not what I meant."

Leo couldn't see what was happening in the room, but she could imagine Mamá's ice-cold stare. She was using her manager voice, the one she used to calm and quiet an upset customer, the perfect mix of stern and polite. Leo had never seen anyone face that tone and that stare without wilting a little.

But Belinda O'Rourke was not just anyone. "I'm not here to grovel, Elena," she responded. "We're not in high school anymore—you can stop acting like a victim."

"You're right, we're not in high school anymore," Mamá snapped back. "But here you are, still trying to copy off my paper because you can't think of your own ideas."

"I knew I shouldn't have come here," Mrs. O'Rourke said. "I knew you wouldn't be any help. I don't know why I let Becky—"

"Help?" Mamá screeched, loudly enough for Leo to move away from the door. "Why would I be interested in helping you?"

Leo bit her lip and rubbed her ear. She didn't know what was wrong with Mrs. O'Rourke, but she felt certain Becky's mom hadn't come to the bakery just to get into an argument with Mamá. She had looked worried and nervous, just like Mamá had been all week, and now they were fighting over nothing instead of talking about their worries.

Making a quick decision, Leo slipped out of the shadows so she was visible again and darted up the hall.

"Isabel," she said, "does your power work through a door?"

"Not particularly well," Isabel said. "Why?"

"I just . . ." Leo cast her eyes around the kitchen and found her nearly cooled scones, pastel icing glaze waiting to coat them. Her brain searched through the old lists of herbs, the ones she had studied and memorized with Caroline. She rushed to the last cabinet and rooted out a tiny glass bottle of primrose oil.

One drop into the yellow icing bag, and then she squished the bag around in her hand, shutting her eyes tight and willing her magic to mix in. She drew zigzag stripes of yellow across the tops of two scones, sniffing to make sure her magic was working. She plopped the two scones onto a plate, frowning as she tried to think of anything else she could add. Bay leaves were in the plain ingredient cabinet, and she ripped up a few and sprinkled them on top of the scones, not knowing if that was enough to activate their magic but making a quiet wish as she ran toward the office.

Mamá and Mrs. O'Rourke were still shouting when Leo knocked on the door, as loud as she dared.

"What is it?" Mamá's voice was dangerously calm.

Leo gulped. "Mamá, my scones are ready. Will you try one?"

There was a long pause, and then the office door opened. Mrs. O'Rourke's mouth was set in a stubborn scowl, and Mamá's cheeks were pink with anger.

"Leo," she said. "Whatever you're doing, now isn't a good time."

Leo held the plate up. "Please, just try one?"

"They smell amazing," Mrs. O'Rourke said. Her stomach gurgled loudly. "And they look picture-perfect. You made these?"

"Better put those away, Leo," Mamá said, "or they'll be the newest item on the Honeybees menu."

"Please try one," Leo said. "I just want to know what you think of them, *honestly*." Her eyes begged Mamá to trust her.

"Leo . . ."

"Well, I'll try one." Mrs. O'Rourke gave Leo a bright, fake smile. "I'm starving."

Mamá broke off a bite-sized piece of the second scone. Both women popped pieces into their mouths, quiet as they chewed.

"This is a great recipe, Leo," Mamá said. "Sometimes I'm amazed by how fast you pick things up. You left them in the oven just a smidge too long, but I love that flavor in the ici—"

Without warning, Belinda O'Rourke burst into loud sobs.

Mamá raised her eyebrows in alarm, and Marisol and Isabel came running.

"What did you do?" Marisol whispered, grabbing the plate with the half-eaten scones away from Leo.

"I'm sorry," Mrs. O'Rourke said. "I'm so sorry. The scones are delicious, sweetie. I'm just not . . . I can't . . ." She fell into Daddy's desk chair, shoulders shaking.

Mamá left the office, then returned with a paper cup of coffee. Mrs. O'Rourke took it, her breath making a sucking noise through her tears.

"I'm sorry, Elena," she said. "I promise, I didn't come here to have it out with you. And I'm not trying to defend . . . Obviously I was wrong back when we were in high school. There was no reason to run against you for class president."

"I didn't care about the election," Mamá said. "I was hurt. You were my friend."

"Honesty spell," Leo whispered back to Marisol.

"I wanted everything you had just because you had it," Mrs. O'Rourke said. "You had the perfect family and the perfect grades and you were so confident about the life you had planned for yourself."

"*You* were the one who went out to conquer the world," Mamá argued.

"Because I was running away," Mrs. O'Rourke said. "I couldn't even come back to Rose Hill until my father passed away. I was afraid. Can you believe he still had that kind of effect on me?"

Leo clapped her hand over her mouth. Mrs. O'Rourke had said that her coming back had to do with "him," but it wasn't about Abuelo Logroño at all.

"I promise, I didn't plan to come back and, you know, steal away your business and your menu. Would you believe me if I said that I honestly forgot about your bakery, at least at first? The idea to sell baked goods just . . . came to me, and before I knew it, I had a space and a website and a whole menu planned, and I swear it must have been subconscious because I never realized . . . I would never have been brazen enough to just copy what you've done. Not anymore, at least."

Mamá laughed. It was totally unbelievable, except when you knew that a brujo who specialized in illusions was part of the story. Leo knew, like Mamá did, that Mrs. O'Rourke's story was true.

But it didn't change anything.

"So, did you come here for confession?" Mamá asked. "That's nice, Belinda, but . . . the damage is done. And I have a bakery to run. I guess we both do."

"But that's why I'm here." Mrs. O'Rourke hiccuped pitifully. "I'm not asking for forgiveness. I'm asking for help."

"I don't know what I can do to help you—" Mamá began.

"I can't bake!"

Mamá looked at Leo, who looked at Marisol, who looked at the plate of scones. Maybe the spell had been too strong. Leo had only wanted to help Mamá and Mrs. O'Rourke to communicate with each other. But she worried she'd inadvertently created some kind of truth serum.

"It's all going wrong," Mrs. O'Rourke said after another bout of tears. "Everyone I try to hire for my kitchen falls through. Three people yesterday said they couldn't find the building. It's not a large town! And the day before that, my back-of-house manager quit because she said the shelves were unsafe; plates and bowls kept falling on her head. And my ovens!

They must have been installed poorly, because I can never get more than one on at a time, and even then everything comes out raw or burned. I'm not a trained professional, but I know I should be able to bake a tray of sugar cookies without disaster!"

"I'm . . . sorry to hear all that," Mamá said. Isabel was tugging Leo's sleeve, eyebrows high on her forehead, and Marisol had a satisfied smirk.

"You know my grandma Kelly?" Mrs. O'Rourke said. "She was a superstitious old bat, but I'm starting to think she knew what she was talking about. I've cursed my business, acting the way I did. And now I want to set things right. The fair folk reward a good deed, right? That's how Grandma Kelly always told it."

Isabel tugged Leo's sleeve even harder, and Leo understood why. The fair folk—that was another name for magical creatures. . . .

The duendes. They hadn't just wished for a way to fix the harm caused by Abuelo Logroño—they had actually gone off to fix it themselves!

"Anyway," Mrs. O'Rourke said, "I need to do something—it's clear that I'm not going to be a success on the back of my baking. I'd rather stick with the tea and honey. That's what I always wanted to do with the café anyway."

"It's a good idea!" Mamá said. "As much as people like to stand around our counter with coffee and gossip, I'm sure they'd love it even more if there was a place to sit and relax."

That did sound nice, now that Mamá put it that way. Leo frowned. If Honeybees wasn't trying to compete with Amor y Azucar, it might even be a place she'd want to go.

"I'm so glad to hear that," Mrs. O'Rourke said. "So will you help me?"

"I'm still not sure what you want," Mamá said.

"I'm sorry." Mrs. O'Rourke waved her hands in the air. "I'm all over the place this morning. I haven't been sleeping well lately—my dog, Bumble, is up all night, barking at nothing. . . ."

Barking at duendes, Leo guessed.

"No, Elena, this is a business proposal," Mrs. O'Rourke continued. "I'm thinking we could both benefit from a partnership."

Mamá stared at Mrs. O'Rourke. "Luis," she called, "can you come in here for a minute?"

"I want to set up a contract with you. I want Amor y Azúcar to provide all the baked goods at Honeybees," Mrs. O'Rourke said. "Some of your classics, maybe a few Honeybees-exclusive pastries? It could be a good way to maintain your traditional brand here while also branching out. And I think I can offer a very fair deal. I'll show you my business plan. . . ." She pulled out her shiny phone and tapped the screen.

Daddy arrived and shooed everyone back to work. Leo iced the rest of her scones (using the nonmagical pink, green, and purple icing) and nibbled nervously on one while the adults talked quietly in the office. Finally the door opened, and Mrs. O'Rourke emerged smiling, followed closely by Mamá and Daddy.

"I'll be in touch," Mamá said. "Why don't you go get some sleep?"

"I'll try," Mrs. O'Rourke said. "If that dog ever stops barking."

"I have a feeling she'll settle down," Mamá said. "It was probably the stress of moving. I'll see you around, Belinda."

"Bye, Elena." Mrs. O'Rourke yawned hugely. "It really is a lovely place you have here."

"I know," Mamá said. "I'm very lucky."

She walked Mrs. O'Rourke to the front door and waved her out.

"Well?" Marisol asked as soon as the door closed. "Are we going to be partners with Honeybees? Did you turn her down just so you could watch her business crash and burn? What happened?"

"Nothing's finalized yet," Mamá said. "We're considering the offer. But it looks like . . . it looks like this could be great for us."

"Like, buy-Marisol-a-car great?" Marisol asked.

"Does this mean the new house is back in the cards?" Alma asked.

"Because we don't want separate rooms," Belén said, "but we are not opposed to an art studio."

"The duendes really saved us," Isabel said. "We'll have to think of a way to thank them."

"Yeah, if only we could save their family from an evil brujo or something," Marisol deadpanned. "Oh, wait."

"If we do take this contract, how big an order will we need to fill every day?" Isabel asked Mamá. "Will you be able to keep up when I leave? Should we hire and train someone new?"

"I'm sure we can handle it," Marisol said. "I mean, I can pick up the slack and start, you know, taking on more responsibilities or whatever." She rolled her eyes as the whole family stared at her. "What? I don't have any plans to leave Rose Hill to learn weird magic like *some people*. So I should probably get used to taking care of things around here, because now it looks like I'll have plenty of job security."

"That's right, you will!" Daddy cheered. The whole family laughed and joked and discussed how they might best transport fresh baked goods across town every day.

In the midst of all the chaos, Leo found JP leaning against a wall.

"I'm a little confused," he whispered. "I don't really get all the business stuff. But if this means the bakery is safe and y'all can buy your new house, then that sounds pretty good to me!"

Leo nodded. "You should come visit once we move in," she said. "We can teach you more baking."

"Thanks—I'll ask my mom!"

"One more thing," Leo said. "Sorry for doing this again, but do you mind if I . . ."

JP reached into his pocket with a sigh. "Hey," he called to the rest of the family, "once this new deal with Honeybees becomes official, does anyone think they might finally get Leo her own cell phone?"

CHAPTER 22
BEYOND

Aunt Rita arrived just in time for Easter mass, and then Uncle Alberto and Aunt Magda and the rest of the cousins met them all at the Logroños' house with delicious-smelling foil-wrapped trays and bowls. Mamá organized the egg hunt. Leo ate ham and pork loin and nopal and mashed potatoes and as much chocolate as she could stomach. The party wound down with Isabel explaining her new college plans to Tía Paloma, Mamá and Daddy explaining their business news to the aunts and uncles and hearing all about Aunt Rita's conference, Marisol picking confetti out of her hair, and JP debating Alma and

Belén about which dragon they'd most like to bond with. Leo took advantage of the lull to slip into the empty kitchen.

She had prepared the syrup ahead of time, and she swiped a heel of old bread from the counter. Her creation baked quickly and was finished before Mamá came in to refill her glass of horchata. When the coast was clear and the ramekin was cool, Leo tucked the tiny card she had made into the tiny dish of capirotada and slipped it into the corner between the refrigerator and the pantry. It was a thank-you note, plus an invitation for the duendes to move into whatever house the Logroños bought in the future. Leo liked having them around and didn't want to accidentally leave them behind in the move.

She didn't see any duendes, but when she checked the corner that night, the ramekin sat empty and clean on the counter, just like all the dishes that had piled up in the sink during the party.

The grand opening of Honeybees in May was the talk of Rose Hill. By the time JP came to visit at the end of July, Leo was already in love with the ginger cinnamon spice herbal tea, which tasted almost like magic smelled. She had also perfected Amor y Azúcar's new honeybee scones. Leo had been tweaking the recipe, with Mamá's help, for months, and they both agreed there was nothing left to improve. Made with Mrs. O'Rourke's highest-quality local honey and sold exclusively at the new location, the scones drew customers like insects to flowers.

Of course, there was a little something extra that kept people coming back.

"I want Honeybees to be a place where everyone can feel comfortable," Mrs. O'Rourke had said in an opening-day interview. "A place for creativity and good conversation. A place to release your worries, and live your truth."

And it was. With the help of their popular scones, people were finding the courage to be honest with each other over honeyed teacups. The café soon became famous around town as the place to go when you needed to have a long chat. Leo couldn't have been prouder.

"Which sounds better?" she asked JP, Caroline, and Brent over a Honeybees table. "Open Secret Scones? Honesty Scones? Friend Scones? Game of Scones?"

Brent stopped, his half-eaten scone inches from his mouth. "Wait, do these things have a truth serum in them? Am I going to blurt out everything I'm thinking?" He clapped his hand over his mouth and glanced at JP.

"No, it's not like that," Leo assured him. "I worked really hard to get the spell just right. It's more like . . . when things are hard, people tend to bottle things up, keep things to themselves. My whole family does it, especially me. This spell doesn't make you blurt out important things. It helps you feel a little bit braver and calmer, so you realize that you don't need to sneak around for no reason. It makes you feel safe to share. To ask for help. To be a friend."

"If it helps you share what you're thinking, then you should really call them Open Book Scones," Caroline said. "I think the lost alliteration is worth it for the increased accuracy."

"You still have a week to decide," Brent said. "I bet we can come up with something better. We'll brainstorm all day. That can be your birthday present! Since I probably won't remember to get you anything anyway." He clapped his hand to his mouth and pretended to stare suspiciously at his scone. "Wow, that was rude. I wonder what could have made me say that."

"Can you invent a Scone of Silence next?" JP asked, throwing a sugar packet playfully at Brent. "I think everyone would really appreciate that."

* * *

"Are you ready?" Mamá asked. She touched the corner of her eye, as if some dust had gotten in it.

"Are you sure about all the spellings?" Tía Paloma asked. "Nothing's worse than trying to squeeze an extra N into 'belladonna,' only to realize that that's the English spelling and you're writing in Spanish and now you have to cross the whole thing out, ruining an otherwise perfect page! I, um, know from experience."

"I'm ready," Leo said, holding a dark pink gel pen above the blank page of the recipe book.

"Then go already," Marisol said, but she smiled and patted Leo's head.

Alma, Belén, and Isabel completed the circle, surrounding Leo in the bakery office as she put pen to paper to add her own original spell to the recipe book.

OPEN HEART SCONES
CAT (OR DUENDE) GOT YOUR TONGUE? THESE HONEY TREATS WILL HELP YOU COMMUNICATE MORE HONESTLY, ESPECIALLY WITH THE PEOPLE YOU LOVE.

"It's perfect," Isabel sighed. "Now let me write the Spanish."

"Let her finish the recipe first." Marisol elbowed her sister. "Jeez."

When the ink was dry on both pages and languages, Mamá closed the book.

"I'm very proud of you, Leonora Elena."

"Me too," Alma said, clapping Leo's shoulder.

"They grow up so fast," Belén added, wiping a fake tear.

"Now there's just one thing left to do," said Tía Paloma.

"There is?" Leo had put her mark in the recipe book, solidifying her place in the family line, giving her knowledge to generations of brujas who would come after her. Her heart was singing and her head felt like it was full of yeast and rising high. What more was left to do?

The office light went out suddenly, and Leo checked the air for magic, but instead she smelled smoke and saw a dim orange glow on the desk. She spun around to see Daddy in the doorway, holding a white frosted tres leches cake with thin candles that Leo recognized as Caroline's handiwork.

Caroline's face glowed in their light, between Brent and Tricia. Mai and Becky stood on the other side of the cake.

The office was way too crowded, but everyone

squeezed in to sing "Las Mañanitas" and "Happy Birthday" anyway. Then they moved to the kitchen so that the cake could be cut and everyone had room to eat.

"Did you wish for something good?" Daddy asked Leo, after giving her head a one-fingered push to send her face-first into her slice of cake.

Leo wiped sugar off her cheek and nodded. She hadn't wished for a present or miracle this year. She already had everything she needed.

She just wished for a future filled with more moments like this.

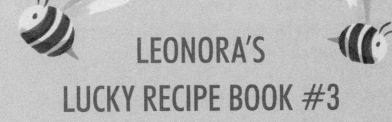

LEONORA'S
LUCKY RECIPE BOOK #3

LOVE SUGAR
MAGIC

LEO'S PIÑATA COOKIES

Use your favorite large animal-shaped cookie cutter! This recipe makes about 6–8 cookies . . . full of surprises!

INGREDIENTS

FOR DOUGH

1 cup granulated sugar

1 cup powdered sugar

1 cup butter

2 eggs

1 cup vegetable oil

5 cups flour

1 teaspoon baking soda

1 teaspoon salt

1 tablespoon vanilla extract

1 teaspoon almond extract

Gel food coloring

FOR INSIDES AND ASSEMBLING

½ cup powdered sugar (for frosting)
2 teaspoons milk (for frosting)
Mini M&M's candies

DIRECTIONS

Cream together the granulated sugar, the pow-dered sugar, and the butter. Then beat in the eggs and add the oil.

Combine all the dry ingredients—flour, baking soda, salt—together and add them slowly to the mixture. Add the vanilla and almond extracts.

Remove the dough from the mixer and let it sit for a few minutes to tighten. Split the dough into five balls of the same size and one smaller ball. Add your favorite food coloring to each dough ball. Make the smallest ball black. Add enough food coloring to each ball to make the color strong and rich.

Use a deep rectangular container roughly the size of your cookie cutter and line it with plastic wrap. Split in half all your balls except the black one. Layer the dough in the container starting with the black dough. Alternate one of each color, pressing down one layer after another, and make sure you have two layers of each color. Cover the dough with plastic wrap and freeze it overnight or for at least five hours.

Remove the dough from the freezer, uncover it, remove it from the container, and unwrap it from the plastic covering. Cut down through the layers, creating striped slices approximately ¼ inch wide, with the black layer on the bottom.

Place them on a baking sheet lined with parchment paper and bake at 350 degrees for 11 minutes.

While the cookies are baking, make the frosting: Mix together ½ cup of powdered sugar and 2 teaspoons of milk. Place in a plastic Ziploc bag and cut off one of the corners to make your own piping bag.

As soon as the cookies are taken from the oven, use your cookie cutter to make the shapes. Each pinata will be three cookies stacked together, creating a three-dimensional figure!

Take your cookie cutter and cut two cookies in one direction and one cookie in the opposite direction by flipping the cookie cutter. This will make sure that when you assemble your piñata cookie, the baked sides (the sides that were browned by the baking sheet) are on the inside of the pinata. Take one of the three cookies and make a rectangular cut in the center. This is the pocket where the M&M's will go. Place the cookies on a rack to cool.

After they've cooled, take the first piñata cookie and lay it upside down so that the baked bottom is facing you. Draw around the edge of the cookie with the frosting mixture, which will help the cookies to stick together. Next, stack the cookie with the hole in it, and add the M&M's to the open pocket. Put another line of frosting glue on the middle cookie.

Finally, place the last piñata cookie—the one facing the other way—on top (so the baked side is on the bottom) to conceal the M&M's inside. Let these sit and harden for at least 40 minutes before you stand them upright.

CAROLINE'S CINNAMONY CHURROS

Makes about 16 cinnamon-sugar churros. Be sure to dunk and dip.

INGREDIENTS

FOR DOUGH

  1 cup water
  6 tablespoons butter
  2 tablespoons granulated sugar
  1 teaspoon vanilla extract
  1 cup flour
  1 teaspoon salt
  2 large eggs
  Vegetable oil (for frying)
  A bowl of cinnamon and sugar

FOR CHOCOLATE DIPPING SAUCE

1 cup heavy cream
1 cup dark chocolate chips
1 teaspoon cinnamon
½ teaspoon salt

DIRECTIONS

In a large pan over medium heat, combine water, butter, and sugar. Bring to a bubbly boil and add vanilla extract. Stir. Turn off the heat and add flour and salt. Stir with a wooden spoon until it turns thick. That will take about 30 seconds. Let the mixture cool for about 12 minutes.

Beat the eggs into the cooled mixture one at a time. Don't rush! Let it all combine. Transfer the mixture to a piping bag with a large star tip.

Using a large pot over medium heat, place enough vegetable oil to come halfway up the sides of the pot and heat to 375 degrees. Hold the piping bag a couple of inches above the oil and carefully pipe churros into 6-inch ropes. Use kitchen scissors to cut off the dough after it leaves the piping bag.

Fry for about 4–5 minutes or until golden. You can fry 3 or 4 churros at a time, but be sure to allow the oil to come back up to temperature for each batch. Remove churros with tongs and immediately roll them in the bowl of cinnamon and sugar.

To make the chocolate dipping sauce, pour heavy cream into a small saucepan and bring to a simmer over medium heat. Place chocolate chips in a medium glass bowl, and pour hot cream over top of them. Let sit for two minutes, then add cinnamon and salt and whisk to combine.

Serve the warm churros with the chocolate dipping sauce.

ACKNOWLEDGMENTS

It's actually surreal to be writing my third set of acknowledgments. After you go through the publishing thing a few times, it's tempting to start taking the process for granted. It's not granted. Every single book is a miracle of collaboration, so I want to thank all the collaborators who made this one possible.

Thank you first and foremost to all the readers. There would be no book three without y'all. Extra bonus Brownie points to the teachers, librarians, and booksellers who have supported and promoted the Love Sugar Magic series from day one.

Dhonielle Clayton and Sona Charaipotra, Victoria Marini, and the whole Cake Literary family, thank you for giving me the chance and the platform to tell these stories. I still can't believe my good luck.

Thanks to my editor, Jordan Brown, who has been such a source of support with both the writing and the other author stuff, and who appreciated all the weird parts of this book.

Thanks to Debbie Kovacs, empress of important things at Walden Pond Press, for all the promotional and moral support.

Thanks to all the folks at HarperCollins and Walden Pond Press who worked on the design, editing, marketing, publicity, important emails, and other miscellaneous tasks to get the book out.

Thanks to Patricia Nelson, my agent, who's helping me plot all my next steps.

Thanks to Mirelle Ortega for once again creating a breathtaking cover. I love everything about it, and you.

Thanks to the writing folks who have been there with helpful tips, sympathetic ears, signal boosts, and virtual hugs. Especially thanks to Las Musas, who are all amazing authors and dedicated supporters of Latinx kidlit.

Thanks to my Rice friends who help me with general freak-outs, my New School friends who help me with writing freak-outs, and my quidditch friends who help me get out of the house and stop freaking out once in a while. Thanks to Ariel for being the first line of defense for all freak-outs and for always checking my Spanish.

Finally, thanks so much my to my family for everything. The constant support and advice and interest and food. It's not a coincidence that the Logroño family is so loving.

(Special shoutout to my brothers and boy cousins, who had to wait until the third book to see any male relative representation.)

Y'all are all superstars, and this series is yours.

ANNA MERIANO is the author of the first two books in the Love Sugar Magic series, *A Dash of Trouble* and *A Sprinkle of Spirits*. She grew up in Houston, Texas, and earned her MFA in creative writing with an emphasis in writing for children from the New School in New York. She has taught creative writing and high school English, and she works as a writing tutor. Anna likes reading, knitting, playing full-contact quidditch, and singing along to songs in English, Spanish, and ASL. Her favorite baked goods are the kind that open hearts. You can visit her online at www.annameriano.com.